LINWOOD BARCLAY

CHASE

Orion
Children's Books

ORION CHILDREN'S BOOKS
First published in Great Britain in 2017
by Hodder and Stoughton

1 3 5 7 9 10 8 6 4 2

A CIP catalogue record for this book is available from the British Library.

ISBN 978 1 5101 0219 4

Printed and bound in Great Britain by Clays Ltd, St Ives plc

The paper and board used in this book are from well-
managed forests and other responsible sources.

MIX
Paper from
responsible sources
FSC® C104740

Orion Children's Books
An imprint of
Hachette Children's Group
Part of Hodder and Stoughton
Carmelite House
50 Victoria Embankment
London EC4Y 0DZ

An Hachette UK Company

www.hachette.co.uk
www.hachettechildrens.co.uk

For Neetha, who never stops believing

PROLOGUE

The moment the White Coat entered the room filled with cages, the prisoner just knew what he was planning. The White Coat was going to kill him.

It might have been the way White Coat man smiled at him through the bars of his cage. The man almost never smiled. He looked at the prisoner through his oversized, black-rimmed glasses. This White Coat was in his fifties, with thinning grey hair. He was a spindly, pale man who spent most of his days sitting at a computer or supervising in the lab, where many of the experiments were conducted and the installations performed. A security card that allowed him to move freely through the building hung around his neck on an elastic strap.

The security card displayed his picture, and his name: SIMMONS.

It made sense to think of him by his actual name. There was only one Simmons, but there were very many White Coats. White Coat men and White Coat women. Some of the others the prisoner had seen over

1

the years were Daggert and Wilkins and the red-haired woman they called Madam Director.

It had been a long time since the prisoner had had a good feeling about any of them. The White Coats were not good people. Oh sure, they fed him and looked after him, trained him. But they did not *love* him.

There'd only ever been two White Coats – that man and that woman – whom the prisoner really believed were his friends. But he hadn't seen them in a long time. A good twelve months now. The prisoner had liked them a lot. He'd liked to hear their stories, and had felt warm all over when they had rubbed and patted his head with affection.

The prisoner was pretty sure something bad had happened to them.

But the more immediate concern was Simmons.

What had caught the prisoner's attention was that Simmons had both hands in the pockets of his long, white coat, as though he was hiding something. The prisoner had a pretty good idea what it might be.

The prisoner moved warily towards the back of his cage.

The other captives must have noticed something was up, too. There were nine others in here, each in his or her own cage. The cages were stacked against the one wall, five in the bottom row, five in the top. Three of the captives began to snarl and bark and pace, although pacing amounted to little more than walking in a tight circle. They had to be picking up the same signals from Simmons as the prisoner.

The prisoner wished he could communicate with his fellow captives, to know what they were thinking. But the White Coats had been careful to disable any sort of sophisticated communication between the subjects, fearing that if they could forge mental links they might band together against the White Coats. The prisoners could still express themselves through whimpers and growls and tail-wagging and raised hackles – the old-fashioned ways – but they'd all moved far beyond that now.

Simmons came to within a foot of the prisoner's cage, smiled – a little bit of spinach visible between his two top teeth – and said, 'How we doin' today? How's my boy?'

The prisoner just stared back at him. It struck him that it might be better not to be confrontational. It would be better not to let Simmons know he suspected anything was wrong. Then again, Simmons was not stupid. Simmons knew that while the prisoner was one of the programme's failures, he still possessed a high degree of intelligence.

It was, after all, the White Coats who had designed and installed all of the prisoner's implants. Right there, on the other side of the room, on what looked like an operating table, with a bank of lights suspended over it, and a dozen monitors on the wall beside it. These were the people who had programmed him to be so much more than just a dog – an animal with talents and abilities light years beyond what he'd come into the world with. When he was little, still just a pup, he could never have dreamt that one day he'd be able to read and understand multiple languages, analyse data, be the eyes and ears for a multi-billion-dollar secret organisation.

When he was a pup, he hadn't dreamt about much more than chasing squirrels.

The White Coats knew that while the prisoner had exceptional abilities, he was deeply flawed. Despite their best efforts, this subject was a failure. His natural instincts could not be suppressed by technology. No amount of software could overrule his canine characteristics. He was, first of all, too distractible. He could not be trusted to stay focused on the task at hand. The White Coats could send him, for example, to sniff out the location of a terror-ist bomb, the lives of thousands hanging in the balance, but if he caught sight of someone tossing around a ball, he'd interrupt his mission to go and chase it.

The prisoner knew this was why the White Coats were going to do something very bad to him.

'Look what I brought you,' Simmons said, taking his left hand out of his pocket. He held something small and dark in his fingers, not much larger than a marble.

A treat.

A beefy, salty, delicious treat.

The prisoner felt his tongue slip from his mouth, running along the sides of his jaw and over his snout. It happened before he'd even realised it. They knew him so well, knew how much he liked these treats. It was one of the prisoner's many weaknesses. They knew just how to turn him against himself.

The prisoner nearly stopped himself from looking eager for the treat, then realised that wagging his tail, which would have been his normal response, was the way to go.

Let the White Coat think he was happy.

Holding it between his thumb and forefinger, Simmons worked the treat through the chain-link grill that separated him from the prisoner.

'Come on,' Simmons said. 'Bet you'll love this. You know how much you like to gobble these down. Yum yum. They're so delicious! I could almost eat one myself. They're your favourite.'

The prisoner raised his head slightly, to within a few inches of the roof of his cage, and sniffed. The man wasn't lying. This treat was definitely among his favourites. His nostrils flared ever so slightly as he took in the smell, almost tasting it.

He kept his tail wagging, but stayed pressed up against the back wall of the cage.

'What is it, sport?' Simmons asked. 'You not hungry? I was hoping you might be. I've got lots more of these in my pocket.'

The prisoner couldn't help but notice that Simmons's right hand was still in his other pocket. His nostrils flared again, taking in more of the essence of the tasty morsel.

There was something wrong with it. He was sure of that now. There was something wrong with the treat.

It did not smell right.

He did not dare eat it. But if he didn't take it, the White Coat Man would suspect the prisoner was on to him.

So he padded to the front of the cage, stretched his furry neck forward, and took the treat gingerly between his teeth.

'There ya go!' Simmons said. '*Dee*-licious!'

It took every bit of strength the prisoner had not to give the treat a couple of quick chews and gulp it down. But he couldn't just let it sit there in his mouth. He had to pretend.

So he made his jaw go up and down twice, then closed his mouth, keeping the treat tucked beneath his long, wet, pink tongue. It would not take long for the treat to dissolve on its own. If he kept it in his mouth long enough for that to happen, he might as well swallow it.

Couldn't do that.

'Starting to feel a bit sleepy there, Chip?' Simmons asked. 'I suspect you will very soon.' He smiled sympathetically. 'I have to tell you, this hurts me more than it hurts you, in a lot of ways. We've grown attached, you and I. We really have. We've been through a lot together. I can't help but think about what might have been, had things worked out.'

Ah, the prisoner thought. *I'm supposed to get sleepy.*

He would play into that. With this tranquilised treat in his mouth, it made sense to fake some symptoms soon. He stood there, cocking his head slightly to one side, as though he really cared what this man had to say.

'It's too bad about you, Chipper. You're a mighty fine dog. You're the kind of mutt anyone'd be happy to have around the house, but that just doesn't cut it here. And it's not like I can just hand you over to some family, let them raise you like a normal dog. Not with everything we've put inside you.'

The prisoner named Chipper blinked. Let his eyes close for half a second, allowed his head to droop.

'I mean,' Simmons said, leaning in close to the cage and whispering so the other animals wouldn't hear, 'we'd have to cut you open and take everything out first, and that'd probably kill you anyway, so this is the way we're going to have to do it. Look at you, getting all dozy. Why don't you just move back a bit there while I open up the cage?'

The prisoner took two steps back, then sat down on his haunches, front legs extended, head lowered. A passive posture.

The cage opened with a squeak of its rusty hinges. Several of the other animals continued to whine and bark. The room smelled of fear and fur.

'That's a good boy,' Simmons said. 'I want you to know this isn't going to hurt. It'll be over before you know it.'

That was when the White Coat man began to withdraw his right hand from his pocket. There was something in it. About six inches long. Narrow and cylindrical.

Shiny at the tip.

The prisoner knew what that was. Any second now, Simmons would be injecting that needle deep into the fleshy part of his hind leg. Forcing down the plunger with his thumb.

Filling him with sweet, instant death.

That's how smart the prisoner was. He knew about all these things. It was Simmons who'd taught him. It was Simmons, and the other White Coats, who'd filled his memory banks with the knowledge of such things. And yet, ultimately, they still thought they were so much smarter than him. They were foolish enough to think he wouldn't figure out what was coming.

Chipper knew much more than they could ever have imagined. He slowly and non-threateningly rose up on all four paws, positioned his hind legs against the back wall of the cage.

'Just hold still there,' Simmons said soothingly, raising his hand with the syringe as the other went to hold him down.

Suddenly, the prisoner drove his back legs hard into the wall, using them like pistons to shoot himself out of the enclosure, a missile with fur.

The poisoned treat slipped out from beneath his tongue a millisecond before his jaws clamped down on Simmons's wrist. He drove the teeth in, causing the syringe to fall and clatter to the tile floor, barely making a sound.

What did make a sound was Simmons. He screamed in horrific pain as the animal's teeth broke skin and pierced an artery. The man fell to the floor, clutching his wrist with his other hand, the dog's jaws still clenched on his arm.

'Help!' he screamed.

The other dogs went into a frenzy. A symphony of canine rage and fury and excitement.

The smell of blood filled the air.

The prisoner was able to read more into the sounds the other dogs made than his human captors ever could. In those barks and snarls he heard anger, fear and more than a hint of satisfaction. All the prisoners here shared contempt for their master captors, these cold people who worked to turn them into high-tech tools.

Chipper relaxed his grip on the man's wrist and turned his attention to the security card hanging around his neck. Simmons jerked back in fear as the dog clamped his teeth on the elastic strap, snapping it so that the card broke away and skittered across the floor.

'Help me!' Simmons screamed again, looking up to the corner of the room where the surveillance camera was mounted. But it was the middle of the day. Chipper hoped no one was watching. Didn't they mostly keep tabs on this room at night, in case agents of some foreign power or a competing agency tried to break in and steal, or kill, the animals? Was it even likely anyone would hear his cries for help over the chorus of barking and growling?

Chipper couldn't get his mouth around the card lying flat on the floor, so he used his tongue to lap it up, as if it were a cracker. Then, once the card was in his mouth, he moved it around, held it gingerly between his front teeth, and ran over to the door while Simmons writhed on the floor, clutching his arm. The card reader was mounted next to the door, about three feet up. The prisoner had watched the White Coats use these cards a thousand times. All they had to do was wave it in front of the small green light that was no bigger than the end of a pencil.

The prisoner raised himself on his hind legs, put his front paws on the wall to steady himself, and positioned the card in front of the light, prompting the door to retract sideways into a pocket in the wall.

As he scooted through the opening, he glanced back to see Simmons struggling to his feet.

'Stop!' Simmons said, scrambling towards the door. 'Get back here, you miserable mutt, or—'

The door whipped shut before Simmons could reach it. And without his card, he couldn't get out.

Chipper sprinted down the long hallway. He knew the way out. They took him and the others outside all the time for exercise and training purposes. As he neared the end of the hall and the next door, he put on the brakes, but the floor was marble and had been waxed overnight, and he slid right into the door with a thump, nearly losing his grip on the security card. He reoriented himself, got up on his hind legs again, waved the card in front of the green light.

The door opened.

Now he was in the main lobby. People – some in white lab coats, others in suits – were briskly walking from here to there, going about their daily rituals. That's the way it was at The Institute. No one dallied. Everyone moved with purpose.

The main door – *the door to The World* – was open. Cool, fresh air wafted into the building between the two retracted glass panels. A million scents from outside – every last one of them smelling of freedom – found their way to his nose.

Everyone stopped. They were not accustomed to seeing one of the subject animals free, unleashed and unattended. They certainly weren't accustomed to seeing one with the fur around its mouth matted with blood, a security card held gingerly between its teeth.

Maybe they'd think he'd been taught a new trick!

Chipper, his eyes on that open door, poured on the speed, allowing the card to slip from his mouth. He didn't need it any more.

'Stop him!' someone shouted.

'Get that dog!' shouted another. 'Don't let him get out!'

The first person yelled, 'Shoot him!'

'Don't be crazy!' said another. 'He's worth a fortune!'

No time to look over his shoulder and see who might be taking aim at him. All he could do now was run.

The glass doors were starting to close. Someone had hit a button.

The prisoner ran faster.

The doors were nearly shut.

Chipper slipped through, the door closing on the tip of his tail. He gave a small tug, and he was free.

He was a prisoner no more. Chipper was free.

But simply getting free was not the point. There was something very important he had to do.

Find the boy.

01

'You call this clean, Jeffrey?' the woman said, pulling back the curtain and inspecting the shower stall. 'This isn't clean.'

'I'm sorry, Aunt Flo,' Jeff said. 'I really scrubbed in there.'

'You know how I can tell it's not clean?' she said. 'When I run some water into the shower, like this.' And she turned on the cold, pulling her hand back quickly so as not to get herself wet. 'You see what the water does when it hits the tiles? It just kind of spreads out. But if that wall were clean and shiny, the water would bead up into drops. Do you see any drops?'

'I see some,' Jeff said tiredly. He'd been awake since six o'clock, before the sun was even up. That struck him as awfully early for a twelve-year-old kid to have to face the world. Especially in the late summer, when there was no school. It would resume in a couple of weeks, and this was the first time Jeff could ever remember looking forward to going back.

Today was a Saturday, which, at one time, was a day when Jeff got to sleep in, and even when he did finally get up, goof off. But it had been a long time since he'd had that kind of Saturday. It was only ten in the morning, but Jeff felt as though he'd been up for days.

Saturday was the busiest day around here at Flo's Cabins. Most people who came to his aunt's fishing camp here on Pickerel Lake, at least in the summer months, stayed for a week at a time, and that week ran from Saturday to Saturday. So on those days, many or all of the eight cabins would be vacated, and new guests would check in. Turnover Day, Aunt Flo called it.

One of Jeff's many jobs on any given Saturday in the summer was to get those cabins cleaned as quickly as possible. Calling them cabins made them sound pretty rustic. And while they were not exactly palaces, each cabin had running water and a proper bathroom with a shower. Of all the jobs Jeff had to do, cleaning the cabins was the one he hated most. You get a bunch of fishermen renting a cabin for a week, and it can be a pretty frightening sight by the time they leave. Scum-caked dishes, half-empty beer bottles with cigarette butts in them, fish guts in the trash can. An amended line from a musical his mom liked ran through his head: 'These are a few of my *least* favourite things!'

But Jeff would rather vacuum a hundred carpets, wash a thousand windows, clean a million stoves, before having to clean one bathroom used by three middle-aged fishermen for an entire week. That was major GBI: Gross Beyond Imagining. Did none of these guys know how to aim? Did they actually wash their hands *before* using the hand towels? Did they even take their muddy boots off before stepping into the shower?

Aunt Flo was a neat freak, so no matter how good a job you did, she'd find fault with it. Like she was doing on this particular Saturday morning, looking into the shower stall of Cabin Four, which was the last cabin Jeff would have to clean today. At least he wouldn't have to clean Cabin Eight, where there would be no turnover. It had been rented for the entire summer by old Mr Green. He pretty much looked after the place himself.

The only good news was, even though Jeff had several cabins to get clean, there were no new guests arriving today, unless someone without a reservation drove in off the main road. That was always a possibility. But it was nearly the end of summer, Aunt Flo explained, and that meant families were getting ready to go back to work and preparing their kids for a return to school.

'I don't think fishermen really care if all the tiles glisten that much,' Jeff said to Aunt Flo as he

15

continued to struggle with the shower. 'As long as it's pretty clean, I think they're okay with it.'

His aunt sighed. It was her favourite sound to make. She'd quickly breathe in, then let the air out long and low, shaking her head at the same time.

'That's your whole thing, isn't it?' she said. 'All it has to be is *good enough*. Well, good enough is not good enough for me. I want things perfect.'

One might have thought, listening to her, that she was running a Hilton hotel instead of a fishing camp.

'Many of these men,' she continued, 'may not care if everything sparkles, but quite a few bring their wives and the rest of their families, and we don't want any of them to think that a cabin rented to them by Florence Beaumont is anything less than pure perfection.'

'Fine,' Jeff said, getting out his sponge and bottle of green cleaning spray and taking another run at it.

Aunt Flo, satisfied that she had defeated her nephew, went off to inspect his work in Cabin One. As the boy scrubbed, the cleanser fumes started getting into his lungs in the confined space of the shower and he thought maybe he'd pass out. *Which*, he thought, *might not be the worst thing in the world. It would be like a mini-vacation.*

At least once he was done here, he'd be outdoors. There were plenty of other chores that would get him out into the fresh air.

Aunt Flo had half a dozen fourteen-foot aluminium boats she rented out, which were tied up at one of several old, wood docks. Jeff had to make sure they were cleaned and respectable. After finishing with the shower, he walked down to the water's edge, a short distance from the cabins, waving some mosquitoes away from his face along the way.

The first boat he looked at made him think someone had been killed in it. The bottom appeared to be filled with gobs of tiny intestines, floating around in an inch of dirty water. But Jeff knew they were worms, or as many of the fishermen liked to call them, 'night crawlers'.

At least the boat didn't have any— oh, yes it did. Someone had cleaned his catch in the boat. Cleaning did *not* mean someone used some Windex and paper towels to make a fish all shiny. Someone had gutted the fish – sliced it open on the underside and pulled out all the insides and dumped them in the bottom of the boat.

This is a really great job, Jeff thought, *if your hobby is barfing.*

But it didn't matter how sick this made him feel. He had to get into the boat and deal with it. There was an old, rusted coffee can tucked ahead of the seat in the bow that he could use to scoop a lot of the mess out.

He stepped in, placing his feet on the seat so as not to ruin his sneakers. He'd done this a hundred times,

17

and was always able to keep his balance, even when the boat shifted beneath him.

But what he didn't know was that there was one squirmy, slimy, slippery worm on that seat, and when his right foot landed on it, it was like stepping on a banana peel.

And before he knew it, he was in the air.

Jeff landed right in the bottom of the boat, thudding against the aluminium hull and creating a small splash. He was covered in dead worms, mud and bits of slimy fish guts.

Jeff shouted a word he was usually careful not to say around grown-ups. If his parents had heard him use it, they'd have chewed him out big time.

Wouldn't that be great? To have parents who'd chew you out big time.

But instead, it turned out to be Aunt Flo, standing right there near the end of the boat launch, who heard him. She might not be happy to hear a twelve-year-old use that kind of language, but what was she going to do? Send him to his room? Who'd do all the chores then?

She stood and looked disapprovingly at Jeff, arms folded across her chest.

Jeff looked from her to his gross hands, a dead worm wedged between two of his fingers. At that moment, a mosquito landed on the tip of his nose, and instinctively, without thinking of the consequences, he slapped at it.

Now, all that stuff he'd been sitting in, including that dead, slimy worm, was splattered across his face.

Aunt Flo let out one of her trademark sighs.

She said, 'Are you going to just goof around all day, Jeff Conroy, or are you going to get some work done?'

* * *

After Jeff cleaned up that boat, and himself, he had to go to the garbage dump. That meant loading up all the cans of trash that had filled up over the week, lifting them up onto the bed of Aunt Flo's old Ford pickup and heading a mile down the road to the local landfill site.

He'd tried to explain to her that, at twelve, it wasn't legal for him to take her truck on the county road that ran past her place, even if Jeff's dad had taught him how to drive on Aunt Flo's fifteen acres when they'd all been up here as a family the year before. Not that there was all that much to it. You just pulled the column shifter over to 'D', put your foot on the gas and away you went.

'That's ridiculous,' his aunt had said when he protested. 'Your legs are long enough to reach the pedals. You're taller than I am, and I don't have any trouble driving the truck. Good Lord, if you're this tall now, I can't imagine what you'll be when you're eighteen. Your father told me you used to go to the go-kart tracks all the time, so I know you know how to drive. And most important of all, that garbage isn't going to walk itself to the dump.'

'But if the police stop and ask for my driver's—'

Aunt Flo waved a hand, dismissing his concerns. 'The police will understand. If they stop you, you tell them I'll rent them a boat for free for the afternoon to go fishing. The police don't do anything anyway. There's no crime around here. They might as well sit out in the lake with their pole in their hands.'

She snickered.

Jeff drove the truck around the camp, loading the full cans. Then he steered the old Ford out to the end of the driveway, where it met the paved road, and where one might see a car every ten minutes. Jeff turned right and headed for the dump.

He looked over at the empty seat next to him and wished that Pepper were there.

Pepper had been his dog. She'd only gotten to ride in this truck once.

She was a four-year-old black and white border collie. Her right eye was surrounded with white fur, her left with black. That one trip she took with him in this truck, at the beginning of the summer, was enough to see she loved it. She'd stick her head out the passenger window, nose into the wind. The only thing she had loved more than the ride to the dump was the dump itself, where she could run about chasing squirrels and rats and seagulls.

If she were there now, she'd be revelling in the scents of the countryside, taking short breaks from the window to dash over and lick his face.

He loved Pepper so much.

But Aunt Flo didn't like dogs, and that was her one condition before agreeing to take Jeff in after his parents died. She would not have that dog living under her roof. Another home would have to be found for her. So a week after Jeff got there, he had to give her to a family back in the city that lived on his street.

Jeff thought about Pepper, and Aunt Flo, and this new life of his, and got so wrapped up in his thoughts that he failed to notice a huge pothole just ahead.

The front right wheel dropped into it.

BANG!

A millisecond later, the back right wheel dropped into it.

BANG!

And then Jeff heard a distant crash. He glanced into the rear-view mirror, and there was one of the garbage cans, on its side in the middle of the road, trash strewn everywhere.

Jeff couldn't leave a mess like that all over the road, so he hit the brakes. But before he got out of the truck to run back up the road to clean up that mess, he touched his forehead to the top of the steering wheel and closed his eyes.

He wanted to cry.

He hated it here.

He hated it here so much.

He missed Pepper.

But even more than Pepper, he missed his mom and dad. Losing your parents when you were just a kid, well, that just sucked.

02

When he first escaped The Institute, Chipper's immediate goal was to put as much distance between himself and the White Coats. Then he could figure out a way to get to his destination.

Legs pumping, he tore across The Institute's lush grounds, heading for the main gate, which was closed. That didn't worry him too much. The gate was designed to keep out people and cars, but there was plenty of room between the bars for him to slip through.

The guard had evidently been given a head's up, because he'd come out of his tiny windowed office, no bigger than a phone booth, and was positioning himself in the middle of the gate, which was a good thirty feet across. He placed his feet far apart, bent slightly at the knees, arms outstretched, looking a bit like a hockey goalie without the pads and mask, clearly thinking he could intercept Chipper.

Chipper aimed himself straight at the guard, then at the last second pivoted left, then right, causing the guard to throw himself in the opposite direction. The man hit the pavement and watched helplessly as Chipper squeezed between two black iron bars and scurried out onto the sidewalk.

Chipper glanced back for a fraction of a second, to see what the guard might do next.

He did exactly what the dog feared he might. He took out the gun he kept holstered at his side, raised it, took aim through the gate, and squeezed the trigger. Evidently he'd not gotten the message that Chipper was too valuable a piece of property to have bullets going through it.

The Institute was situated on a large piece of land, and once inside the compound, there was a sense of being in the country. It offered a rural, tranquil feeling, at least for those who were able to roam the grounds and were not kept in cages in windowless rooms, yet it was actually situated within the city, occupying an entire block. The streets surrounding it were filled with cars and buses and taxis, the sidewalks cluttered with pedestrians.

Which was why, when that shot rang out, and the bullet hit the sidewalk just to Chipper's left, ricocheting off the cement, several people screamed and dived out of the way. Chipper altered his course, hugging the buildings, where the guard wouldn't be able to see him until he was well outside the gate.

By that time, Chipper would be at the corner.

When he got there, he turned left then darted out into the street. A bus screeched to a stop as Chipper cut across several lanes of traffic. Once on the other side, the dog spotted an opening, then a set of stairs.

Chipper glanced up, saw the sign. SUBWAY.

He had been equipped, during his time with the White Coats, with a great many talents. Being able to recognise words and letters from more than a dozen languages was actually one of the simpler ones. Just one of many things he'd been outfitted with.

Chipper bounded down the stairs into the underground concourse, weaving his way between people coming out and going in. He ducked in front of a young man carrying a skateboard and zipped under the turnstiles.

'Hey!' someone yelled.

The dog kept going. Echoing from below, the whooshing sound of a train pulling out of the station. By the time Chipper arrived at the platform, the train was gone. He glanced left, at the southbound line, then right, at the northbound. He would take whatever train arrived first.

He regularly glanced back up the stairs, wondering if he had been followed. The White Coats wouldn't be able to keep up with him on foot. He ran too quickly for them. There was probably a team heading to The Institute's garage, where they kept a fleet of big, black SUVs.

The dog looked at the other people on the platform and sniffed, his nose overwhelmed with their smells and the scents of the subway itself. Oil and metal and soot and dirt. He figured if there were anyone down here from The Institute – one of the actual White Coats, or the other ones who went around in dark suits – he'd catch a whiff of them. The Institute had a bleachy, antiseptic aroma about it. Chipper had heard workers say they couldn't get the stink off them, even after they'd gone home.

The dog heard a distant rumbling.

Chipper peered into one of the tunnels and saw a headlight. He knew all about subways and other kinds of transportation. Learning how to use various modes of travel had been part of his training. There'd been countless days out 'in the field', as the White Coats liked to call it. Riding in cars, on buses, getting onto trains, commercial jets. There'd even been a trip in a motorcycle sidecar. Once, he'd gone with one of the White Coats on a hang-glider.

That was fun.

He liked open-windowed cars and motorcycles and hang-gliders best, because he could feel the wind blowing over his face, the hundreds of outdoor scents tantalising his very sensitive nose.

Chipper wasn't sure how long he'd stay on once he'd boarded the subway car. Not to the end of the line. Maybe a few stops, then hop off. He might cross the platform and get on the southbound line, double back, confuse anyone who might be following him.

The train had nearly come to a stop when Chipper saw the rat.

A rat!

A grey rat, nearly a foot long – not counting the tail, which added several more inches to its slithery length. It was scurrying along where the wall at the platform's end met the floor.

No, must resist. Forget about the rat. Stay focused. You must get away. You cannot worry about some stupid rat but it's so big and it's right THERE AND I HAVE TO CATCH IT!

Chipper bolted after the rat.

He hadn't seen any rats at The Institute. Within its walls, it was clean to the point of sterile, certainly free of rodents. Chipper had rarely even seen a spider there. But when they would take him outside for training, he encountered squirrels and chipmunks and birds, and whenever he did, no matter what exercises his trainers were putting him through at the time, he took off after them. Which was exactly why the White Coats were trying to put him down. Well, they weren't here right now, were they? At least, not yet.

Chipper reached the wall just as the rat went around the edge of the platform, into the tunnel, finding a tiny outcropping no more than an inch wide along a row of bricks. Chipper craned his head around, watched the rat getting away from him. Frustrated, he barked at the tiny animal twice, as though that would persuade it to surrender and come back.

Nuts, Chipper thought. The rat would not be his.

He whirled around.

The train was leaving the station.

If a dog could kick itself, that's what Chipper would have done at that moment. No wonder they were scrubbing him from the programme. There were times when he just could not keep his head in the game.

Now he'd have to wait for another train. He'd lost valuable escape time, all because of some stupid little rat.

Dumb!

Chipper padded around the platform and parked himself behind a pillar, thinking he could not be seen. But anyone coming down the escalator to catch a train would see the black and white butt end of a dog sticking out from behind the pillar.

It was hard to hide behind a post when you were constructed horizontally instead of vertically.

Chipper heard a train approaching on the opposite track. Seconds later, it slid into the station and the doors parted. People standing on the other side of the platform waited for passengers to disembark, but not Chipper. He darted onto the car, found himself a spot under one of the benches, and took a moment to catch his breath.

The doors closed. The train began to move. Posters, faces, huge tiles bearing the station name, slid past the windows. Then, beyond the windows, darkness.

Chipper took a moment to assess his surroundings. The car was barely half full. It was neither morning nor late afternoon, so this was not a rush hour crowd. At the far end of the car, a man in tattered clothing who gave every indication of being homeless – the wonderful number of scents coming off of him was one clue – was holding out his grey and dirty hand, asking people for money. Most acted as though he was invisible, looking into their laps, pretending not to see him.

At the other end of the car, closer to Chipper, a young woman was playing a musical instrument. It looked like a violin, but was much bigger. Chipper locked his electronic, million-dollar eyes on the instrument, scanned images in his database. Ah! This was a cello. By the woman's feet, blocking an entire seat that would have held three people, lay the case for the instrument, open to allow people to toss in money if they enjoyed her playing.

As the man begging for money approached and glanced down into the cello case, the woman stopped playing and eyed him fiercely.

'Don't even think about taking my money, Jack,' she said.

The homeless man turned and started walking back to the other end of the car.

Then, suddenly, Chipper's view was blocked.

A woman with very thick legs and a large shopping bag dropped down onto the seat above him. When the dog tried to work his snout between her ankles so he could see what was going on, she let out a startled scream.

She looked down to see what furry thing had touched her, probably fearing it was a rat like the one Chipper wanted to chase, and when she saw that it was a dog, she laughed. Chipper took in her upside down face, which was round with a bulbous nose.

'Hey you,' she said. 'Howya doin'?'

Chipper's tail thumped twice. No matter how dire his situation, he always enjoyed it when people talked nicely to him.

'You're a pretty dog,' the woman said. 'You're *such* a pretty dog. How'd you get on here? You belong to someone?'

She asked nearby passengers if any of them owned this dog.

'Not mine,' said someone.

'Nope,' said the woman who'd been playing the cello.

'So who do you belong to, then?' the woman asked, returning her attention to him. 'Maybe there's something on your collar that says who you are.'

She reached down, tried to grab hold of the ring around Chipper's neck and managed to drag him out from under the seat far enough that she could get a look at it.

He did not want her looking at his collar. She absolutely should not look at his collar. He knew that he might have to snap at her if he couldn't pull himself away. He didn't want to have to do that. He could still taste Simmons's blood in his mouth, and he didn't want to have to bite anyone else.

The woman was trying to get her fingers under the collar, but she couldn't. It was as though the collar was glued to his fur. It seemed attached to his body.

'Someone sure has put that tight on you there, buster. And what the heck is this? It's not a leather collar. It's like it's made out of metal or something. Who'd put a metal collar on a dog?'

Chipper tried to pull his head away but the woman would not let go of him.

As the train rounded an underground curve in the track, the metal wheels squealed and the lights flickered, going out for nearly three seconds before coming back on.

'I've never seen anything like this,' the woman said. 'It's like this collar is welded onto you. And what – what the heck is *that*?'

Maybe he was going to have to bite her after all.

'Is that something . . . is that something you plug something into?' To the passenger next to her, the woman said, 'Doesn't that look like one of those openings like on your phone, when you plug in the wire to recharge it? Why would he have one of those on his collar? That is totally—'

Chipper said, '*Grrrrr.*'

The woman quickly withdrew her hand. 'Whoa! That's not nice! Bad dog! That's a bad dog!'

Chipper scurried back under the seat.

'If you don't belong to somebody,' she said, 'somebody needs to do something with you. You need to go to the pound!'

Chipper didn't like the sound of that, but hoped that if he stayed under here and kept to himself, the woman would leave him alone, at least until they reached the next stop, at which point he'd shoot out those doors the second they opened.

Wouldn't matter which station it was, Chipper would be able to find his way. All he had to do was stop a moment, access his GPS program.

Those folks in the White Coats had thought of everything.

The train clattered along the underground tracks, nothing but black whipping past the windows. The lights inside the car flickered, went off again for a second, and came back on. No one took much notice.

They'd be pulling into another station soon, he was sure of that.

But then the train began to slow. Within a few seconds it had come to a stop in the tunnel, between stations, where it sat in silence for several minutes.

Uncertainty bordering on alarm began to sweep through the car. People from one end to the other began to chatter, speculating as to the cause of the delay.

Chipper could hear them all.

'What's going on? Why is the train stopped?'

'What's happening?'

'Maybe one of the switches is stuck!'

'Hope we're not here long.'

'Why don't they tell us what the problem is?'

Then, a loud crackling over the speakers.

'Attention,' a man said through the static. 'Attention. Sorry for the inconvenience this delay is causing to your journeys. We're going to be here for just another moment. There is no cause for alarm. We do have an incident on the train, but there is, I repeat, no cause for alarm. We will be moving shortly, but when we enter the next station, the doors will not be opening immediately. Repeat, the doors will not be opening immediately.'

The passengers grumbled.

Chipper lay there under the seat, his chin resting on his paws, his brown eyes darting up and around warily.

They know, Chipper thought. *They know I'm on the train, and they're coming to get me.*

03

At the dump, another truck pulled in next to Jeff's as he was emptying the last can of garbage. Painted on the side were the words: SHADY ACRES RESORT.

Jeff knew the place. It was another fishing camp just down the lake from Flo's Cabins. To call it a 'resort' was pushing it. It was a collection of cabins as old and run down as Flo's were. But fishermen – and often the family members they brought along with them – weren't all that picky. As long as they had a roof over their heads, a place to lay their heads at night, a boat that didn't leak, and the fish were biting, they were happy. And even if the fish weren't biting, if the fridge was stocked with cold beer, they'd be okay.

Jeff had driven past Shady Acres a few times in his twelve-foot-long aluminium boat, but he'd never set foot on the place. It was one of Aunt Flo's rare kind-nesses that she let Jeff have his own boat to run around in, which he took out onto Pickerel Lake for a spin whenever he had a few free minutes. But he never took out the boat to fish. Jeff *never* fished. He just cranked up the ten-horsepower motor as fast as it would go and bombed around, making sharp turns, looking for waves tall enough that he could fly over the top of them, hoping to hear the roar of the propeller catching air.

One thing he'd never noticed when buzzing past Shady Acres was the person getting out of the passenger side of that resort's pickup truck right now.

A girl. About twelve or thirteen years old. Skinny, straight brown hair to her shoulders, wearing ratty jeans and sneakers and a faded red T-shirt that said 'SHADY ACRES'.

Getting out of the driver's side was a man Jeff guessed was her dad. Pretty old, maybe even forty. Heavyset, balding, in a plaid shirt and dark work pants.

The girl got to the back of the truck first and dropped the tailgate. Then she jumped up and started moving the garbage cans towards the back. Her dad grabbed them, upended them to allow the trash to drop into the huge pit, then set the empties to one side.

She was pretty strong, Jeff thought, for a girl. Especially a girl who was about the same age he was. He noticed her arm muscles tense and strain as she shifted the cans around. She glanced at Jeff, standing in the bed of his aunt's pickup.

'What are you lookin' at?' she asked.

'Nothing,' he said, turning away. Time to get behind the wheel and head back to Flo's Cabins.

'Where are you from?' she asked.

He turned his head, told her the name of the place.

'Oh,' she said.

Her father said, 'Yeah, I know your spot. That's Flo Beaumont's place. Been running it ever since her husband passed away, about six years ago.' The man smiled at Jeff. 'I heard she got her nephew helpin' her. That you?'

'Yes, sir.'

He nodded. 'I'm John Winslow. This here is my daughter Emily.'

'I'm Jeff Conroy.'

'How old are you?' Emily asked in an accusatory tone.

'Huh?'

'You can't be old enough to drive. How can you be driving? You don't look any more than twelve.'

'Excuse me?' he said. 'I'm not twelve. I'm *sixteen*.' But his voice practically squeaked as he said it, and he knew the girl was never going to believe him. But you had to be sixteen to drive legally, and he didn't want her father reporting him to the police. He seemed like a nice guy, but still. Jeff wasn't so sure Aunt Flo was right about being able to buy off the cops with a free boat rental.

'Seriously?' she said.

37

'What are you?' he asked, determined to be just as insulting. '*Nine?*

'I'm thirteen,' she said, trying to make it sound important.

Jeff smiled. 'Well, maybe in three years, your dad will let you drive the truck. Maybe even by yourself, one day.'

'Nice to see you two hitting it off,' Mr Winslow said. He'd continued emptying trash cans while his daughter and Jeff sparred. 'You gonna help me, Emily, or you just going to flirt with that boy all day?'

Her face flushed with embarrassment. Jeff's did, too. *Flirting?* Jeff was pretty sure what they'd been doing was not flirting.

'*Dad,*' Emily said. She turned away from Jeff to help her father while Jeff got back into the cab of his aunt's old Ford. He turned the key and drove out, glancing into the oversized mirror bolted to the door along the way.

The girl looked his way once, then, maybe afraid Jeff had seen her in the mirror, spun around again.

Sheesh, Jeff thought. The very idea, that beneath all those insults they had taken some kind of instant liking to each other.

But it was nice to know her name was Emily.

04

'Tell me *exactly* how this happened,' Madam Director said sternly to Simmons. The Institute scientist had been released from the infirmary, where his bitten wrist had been bandaged.

The Director, a slim, striking woman with red hair, oversized, black-framed glasses and deep, penetrating eyes, was sitting in a black leather and chrome chair behind a broad aluminium desk that had nothing on it but a paper thin computer monitor and a keyboard.

'He must not have eaten the treat,' a sweating Simmons said. 'He just pretended to eat it. If he'd eaten it, he would have been sleepy enough that I could have injected him.'

'So you were outsmarted by a dog,' Madam Director said, her voice icy and patronising. Simmons had always thought her voice sounded like teeth tearing into flesh.

Defensively, he said, 'Well, Madam Director, not just any dog. As you know, all the canines here are much more advanced than your typical dog. They are, quite frankly, as intelligent as, say, a child of ten or eleven, and—'

'Would you be proud to be outwitted by a child, Simmons?' Madam Director asked.

Simmons swallowed. 'No, ma'am.'

'Which subject was this again?'

'It was animal H-1094, sir— I mean, Madam Director. The one we call Chipper. He was not working out, which is why I was going to inject him, to end his life functions, which would allow us to remove all the hardware and install it in another subject without risk of damaging it.'

'Not working out? Refresh my memory.'

Simmons struggled for an explanation. There was a long one, about how the animal's original instinctive functions were not interfacing satisfactorily with the circuitry, how the software was not successfully over-ruling some of the dog's natural tendencies, how the dog was unable to reliably commit to mission objectives.

But there was a simpler explanation.

'Chipper liked to play,' Simmons said.

Madam Director shook her head. 'And is it true that this *Chipper* actually used your security card to make his way out of the building?'

Simmons cleared his throat. 'Yes, that is what he did. In some ways, however, that is evidence of just how successful the programme is, that a dog could be smart enough to understand—'

Madam Director cut him off with a wave of the hand. 'You're embarrassing yourself, Simmons.'

'Yes, Madam Director. But we're doing everything we can to recover the animal. Just before I came in here I heard that they had it cornered in a subway car. It's only a matter of time before we have it back.'

'Hmm,' said Madam Director, who pushed back her chair and stood up. In four-inch heels, she was taller than he was; her eyes stared down into his. 'And what sort of orders have been given to those in pursuit?'

'To get the dog back, even if it means the hardware is compromised. If the only way to get the dog is to destroy the dog and everything that has been implanted in it, then that is acceptable. It's totally understood that we do not want the dog to come into anyone else's hands.'

'I should think not,' Madam Director said. 'That would be nothing short of catastrophic. Do you realise how few people are even aware of the work we're doing?'

'I have a pretty good idea, yes.'

'Were you aware that not even the President of the United States knows of the work we are engaged in?'

'Yes, Madam Director,' Simmons said.

'The billions of dollars that have been channelled to our research don't even show up on the books,' she

41

said, stepping away from her chair, slowly coming around the desk. 'We are so secret that even the people who are supposed to know about us don't know about us. But when you let that dog outwit you, you put all that in jeopardy. You run the risk of having everything we do here exposed.'

'I, uh, am deeply sorry about that,' Simmons said.

Madam Director stood directly in front of Simmons, close enough that she could smell onions on his breath. Her right hand was closed into a fist, hiding something.

'I can assure you that nothing like this will happen again,' he said.

The woman nodded. 'No, it will not.'

There was a long, awkward pause. Finally, Simmons said, 'Is that all, Madam? Because I'm eager to return to supervising the recovery mission.'

'You don't have to worry about that,' Madam Director said. 'I've already put someone else in charge.'

Simmons's eyebrows went up. 'But I can handle that.'

Madam Director smiled. 'I think Daggert is more the man for the job. I have something else for you.' She opened her right hand to reveal a dark, marble-sized item. It was a beefy, salty treat, just like the one Simmons had given to H-1094.

Madam Director held it up a few inches away from Simmons's lips.

'Eat this,' she said.

'What?'

'Eat. This.'

'Madam Director, really, there's no need to—'

Behind him, he heard the door to Madam Director's office retract into the wall. He spun around and saw a man standing there. He wasn't wearing a white coat like most of the others at The Institute. He was decked out in a black business suit, with a crisp white shirt and black tie. On his feet were black shoes that reflected the lights recessed into the ceiling. He was tall and thin, and one had the sense of being watched by him, even with his eyes obscured by sunglasses.

'Daggert,' Simmons said. 'Just back from the Matrix?'

The man called Daggert said nothing. But Simmons noticed that he held, in his right hand, a syringe.

'Look at me,' Madam Director said.

Simmons looked at her and gulped. 'I'm very, very sorry about what happened.'

'Eat this,' Madam Director said for a third time.

Simmons looked at his boss, then at Daggert and the syringe in his hand. He took the treat, and with great reluctance, placed it in his mouth and grimaced.

'You're thinking that maybe you're just as smart as the dog,' Madam Director said. 'That you can just hide it in there.' She smiled. 'Chew it up.'

Simmons's jaw did not move.

'Come on now, Simmons. I'm doing you a favour. You won't feel a thing. Any other way is going to be much more painful.'

'But . . . but you need me. I'm invaluable!'

Madam Director looked past Simmons to Daggert. 'Who's invaluable, Daggert?'

'Only you,' he said.

She smiled. 'There you have it. Start chewing, Simmons.'

His jaw slowly began to move. Madam Director leaned in close to hear crunching within the man's mouth.

'That's good. Eat that up.'

'Please,' Simmons said as he continued chewing. 'I'm going to make this right. I am. You don't have to . . . put me . . . to sleep.'

Madam Director waved a finger in his face. 'It's not nice to talk with your mouth full.' She smiled. 'As you've probably guessed, that little morsel is a lot more powerful than the one your dog failed to eat.'

Simmons could already feel himself growing weary.

'Swallow,' she said.

Simmons chewed the last of the treat and allowed it to move down his throat. The room began to sway. He reached for the desk to try and steady himself.

His legs grew weak and he collapsed to the floor. Daggert strode further into the room and knelt beside Simmons. He tested the syringe, shooting a couple of

44

drops out the end of the needle, then plunged it through Simmons's white sleeve and into his arm.

'Thank you, Daggert.' Madam Director returned to her chair. 'Remove him. He clashes with my décor. And Daggert?'

'Yes, Madam.'

'We have people in the field already, but I'm putting you in charge of getting that dog back. Take Bailey and Crawford with you.'

'With pleasure,' he said, dragging Simmons from the room.

05

Chipper remained crouched under the seat in the subway car, wondering when they would start moving again. He knew the car couldn't sit in the tunnel indefinitely.

The train began to move.

Chipper thought back to what had been said over the public address system. When they came into the next station, the doors would not be opening immediately. That meant the authorities would be able to board the train and go through it car by car, looking for him.

He had to get off the train.

The wheels squealed and the lights flickered.

That voice came on again.

'Attention, passengers. We are almost at the station. Please remain seated. We will be opening the doors one car at a time while security moves through the train. Please do not be alarmed. This is a standard security precaution.'

Someone said, 'I wonder what's going on?'

The cello player stopped playing. The homeless man continued to ask people for money.

If they were opening the cars one at a time, that had to mean these so-called 'security' people would be starting their search at one end of the train, and as they passed through each car, they'd release the passengers. Which meant Chipper wouldn't be able to get out of this car until it had been searched.

The dog was in the third car from the front.

The wheels squealed again. Much louder this time.

The lights flickered.

And then went out.

One second.

Two seconds.

Three seconds.

The lights came back on.

The dog was gone.

* * *

Moments later, the train rolled into the station. People on the platform crowded up to the doors, expecting them to open, but they did not.

The three men who boarded through the front door of the first car didn't look like transit police. They wore dark suits, white shirts and ties, and very stern expressions. And if one looked closely, one could see a slight bulge under their jackets, just below their shoulders. Each man had a wire coming up out of his jacket to a small device tucked into his ear.

'Everyone remain calm,' the first man shouted to the anxious passengers. The three men scanned the car as they walked through it. They looked mostly at the floor and under the seats.

They went from one end of the car to the other, at which point the first man touched the device in his ear and said, 'First car clear.'

The doors opened and the passengers who wanted off at this station bolted for the platform.

The three men moved slowly through the second car, and when they did not find what they were looking for, the all-clear was given for those doors to be opened. Again, some people disembarked, and others got on.

Now, here they were in car number three.

The homeless man, who was standing at the far end of the car near the woman with the cello, approached, bearing a toothless grin.

'You guys got any spare change?' he asked.

The first man pushed him aside and he toppled into an empty seat. If any of the other passengers in this car had thought about asking what was going on, that was enough to dissuade them.

The three men in suits stopped in the middle of the car, scanned their eyes from one end to the other, then bent to check under the seats. Nothing.

The second man asked the first, 'How many cars are there?'

'Seven.'

'He must be further up.'

They proceeded to the end of the car, and just before they passed through into the fourth, the first man touched his ear again and said, 'Clear car three.'

The doors opened.

Several people exited the train. The thick-legged woman who had taken a seat above Chipper grabbed her bag and headed for the door.

But this was not the stop for the woman who had been playing her cello. She hadn't wanted the homeless man to take the few coins that had been tossed into her case when the lights went out, so she had gently tapped the lid and closed it when everything had gone dark.

Intending to resume playing, and with any luck, take in some more money to help her pay for her music lessons, she leaned to open the case once more.

Like a jack-in-the-box, Chipper sprang from the case and slipped between the doors to the subway platform in the instant before they closed.

But he was not quite quick enough.

The doors had closed on his tail. Three inches of Chipper was still in the train. He went to run and was stopped short. He looked back and saw the problem.

Some of the passengers who'd remained on the car could see his predicament, and were shouting.

49

Chipper couldn't hear what they were saying, but he was worried all the noise they were making was going to draw those black-suited men, now searching car number four, back to car number three.

And what if the train began to move?

Chipper would be dragged by the train into the tunnel, dangling from the door, slammed up against the walls.

One of the passengers filled the windows of the double doors. It was the homeless guy! He dug his fingers in between the doors and struggled to pry them apart.

Chipper tugged hard, but his tail remained trapped.

The man grimaced, his eyes squeezed shut, and he put everything he had into pulling the doors apart.

For a fraction of a second they parted no more than a fraction of an inch. But Chipper was pulling with everything he had at that moment, and he tumbled forward and rolled as his tail came free.

He was stunned, briefly, but then he was on his feet again. But before Chipper ran for the stairs, he looked back at the man in the subway car window and gave him a wag of thanks with his slightly mangled tail.

06

Jeff was heading down towards the lake, thinking maybe he could sneak away for a few minutes in his boat, when he heard a woman shouting, 'Fire!' That was followed quickly by a man yelling: 'Oh, no! Oh, no!'

All the commotion sounded like it was coming from around cabins Four or Five. He started running in that direction. When he came around to the side of the cabins, he saw what was going on.

The couple renting Cabin Four had set up a barbecue on a picnic table just under the overhanging branches of a big pine tree. There were flames shooting three feet into the air, licking at the branches. Both the man and the woman were standing several feet back, frozen, unsure what to do.

Jeff knew one thing was for sure. Something had to be done quickly, because once those flames caught those pine needles, that tree would go up in a flash. And once it was on fire, how many seconds would it take for it to spread to other, nearby trees and the cabin itself? The whole camp could be burned to the ground before the closest fire department – which was miles away in Canfield – could get here.

Jeff's mind raced. He glanced at the lake, which was only about thirty feet away. There was a whole lot of water there. The question was, how would he get it to the barbecue?

Jeff's boat had a bailing can in it. An old coffee can, like his aunt had put into all the rental boats. One large can of water might be enough to douse that barbecue. Jeff ran to the dock, jumped into the boat, grabbed the can, dipped it into the lake and filled it to the brim. Then he leapt back onto the dock and started running towards the flames.

And promptly tripped over his own feet.

Jeff hit the ground hard, the coffee can slipping from his hand, the water spilling out.

The flames were inches from the pine branch. Jeff chastised himself for his clumsiness and stupidity. He was going to have to grab the empty can, run back to the lake, fill it a second time, and—

'Stand back!'

It was Mr Green, the man who rented Cabin Eight for the entire summer. In his hand was a red fire extinguisher. Not as big as one you might find in a school hallway behind glass, but big enough. The couple took several steps back as Mr Green raised the extinguisher, pointed it at the out-of-control barbecue, and buried it in foam with a loud *Froosshhh!*

The flames vanished instantly.

Jeff got to his feet as the woman shouted at Mr Green, 'You just put chemicals all over our hot dogs!'

That made Jeff crazy. Before Mr Green could say anything, Jeff unloaded with, 'You nearly set that tree on fire! Are you people nuts? You set up a barbecue under a tree?'

The couple looked at Jeff, stunned that a kid would talk to them that way. The man said, 'We're going to have a word with your aunt, young man. You talk to us like that, we've got a good mind not to come here ever again!'

'Good!' Jeff said. 'That means our camp might not burn to the ground!'

'Hey,' Mr Green said, gently putting a hand on Jeff's shoulder. To the couple, he said, 'I think now that everything's under control, we can all go back to what we were doing. Sorry about those hot dogs. I might have a few extra in my fridge.'

The couple grumbled something about having more wieners of their own. The woman went back into the cabin while the man dragged the table out from under the tree.

Mr Green said to Jeff, 'You okay?'

'I guess.'

'Come join me on the porch.'

He led Jeff to his cabin, opened the spring-loaded screen door, and pointed to a folding aluminium chair with fraying canvas webbing. 'Sit.'

Jeff sat.

'You're way too young for me to offer you a beer. How about a Coke?'

Jeff said he'd like that, thanks. He was feeling kind of shaky. He didn't yell at grown-ups very often.

Mr Green came back out of the cabin with a can of pop and a bottle of beer. The man was probably in his sixties, and from what Jeff knew, was a retired construction worker whose wife had died a few years ago. He was enjoying his summer here, fishing and reading books and just taking it easy. He was a short, stocky man, with a few wisps of hair around the side of his head, and he wore glasses with thin, wire frames.

'You okay?' he asked, sitting next to Jeff in another folding chair.

'I guess.' The truth was – and he was embarrassed to be feeling this way – he felt like he was going to cry.

'If those people rat you out to your aunt, I'll tell her what really happened,' he said. 'Those two, putting a barbecue under a tree – they're dumb as a pair of old boots.'

Jeff sniffed. 'Thanks, Mr Green.'

'How many times this summer have I told you to call me Harry?'

'My aunt says it's disrespectful because I'm a kid and you're, well, you're sort of old.'

'Well, your aunt ain't here right now, so you call me Harry.'

Jeff smiled. 'Okay . . . Harry. Thanks for the Coke, and for putting out the fire. I might have been able to do it if I hadn't tripped on my own stupid feet.'

'Good thing I keep an extinguisher in my truck. I was sitting on the porch here, reading my John Grisham book, when I saw that idiot putting half a can of lighter fluid on that thing and then *poof!* Up it went. I ran to my truck about the same time you showed up.'

Jeff nodded. He was feeling a lump in his throat.

'You okay, son?' Harry asked.

'It's just – it's, it's. . .'

'You know what I think? I think you're something.'

'What? What do you mean?'

'I mean, here you are, just a kid, helping your aunt run this place. Not having – you know – a mom and dad any more. That was a terrible thing, them dying in a plane crash and all.'

Jeff looked at him. 'You know about that?'

'Your aunt told me.'

'Oh,' he said.

'That's a pretty tough thing to go through. That's why I think you're something. I don't know that I could have dealt with all this when I was your age. How old are you, anyway?'

Jeff wasn't going to lie to Harry Green the way he had tried with Emily. 'Twelve.'

'Ha!' he said. 'The way I seen you driving around in your aunt's truck, I figured you might be a bit older, but not old enough to be driving legally. You're a good driver.'

'Thank you.'

'I've got a son, you know,' he said. 'But he's all grown up, got kids of his own now. Lives clear across the country. Haven't seen him in years.' His eyes softened. 'When he was your age, we did lots of things together.'

Harry sat back in his chair and drank his beer. 'I know I've asked you before, but you should come fishing with me some time. But you don't care much for it, do you?'

'Not really,' Jeff said. 'It's boring, just sitting in a boat all day.'

Harry laughed. 'I suppose. But when you're an old guy like me, boring can be kind of nice. Well, if you ever change your mind and want to come out with me one day before the end of summer, you just let me know.'

'Okay.' Even though Jeff didn't care about fishing, he thought hanging out with Harry Green might be nice. It would be good having someone like him to talk to. Jeff missed both his parents, but he missed them in different ways. He had liked to talk to his mom when he had trouble with his friends, or needed advice about school. With his father, it was more guy stuff. Cars and action movies and baseball and hockey. Things his mom wasn't as interested in. Well, except hockey. His mom had loved hockey. She'd had an uncle who'd once played for Boston. Maybe, Jeff thought, if he went fishing with Harry, if he got to know him a bit, they could talk about those kinds of things, so that it didn't get so boring waiting for a fish to bite the hook.

'You want something to eat?' Harry asked. 'I got some of the sticky buns from that bakery in town.'

'No, thank you. I better go. I was going to go for a boat ride, but I don't think there's time now. I've got to cut some grass.'

Harry Green nodded. 'Your aunt, she works you hard.'

'I guess.'

'It may seem like she's being mean to you, but she's making you tough. You need to be tough in this world.'

'I guess.'

'You guess, you guess, you guess.' He pointed his finger into Jeff's chest, gave it a nudge. 'You have to *know.*'

'Know what?'

'You have to know that you are being the best that you can be. That you're living up to your potential.'

'Okay.'

Harry Green grinned and rubbed the top of his head, mussing the boy's hair. 'Go on with you, then. You ever need help with anything, you just come get me.' He smiled. 'I'm gonna keep my eye on you.'

07

The dog ran.

And ran.

Chipper was moving so quickly his body had moved aerodynamically lower to the ground, like a race-car. The fur on his stomach brushed the surface of the subway concourse floor.

At first, all he wanted to do was get away. Get out of the subway station. Put some distance between himself and those people from The Institute searching the train.

But once he'd emerged from below ground and slipped in among the hundreds of people walking the sidewalk, he headed northeast. He had to get to his destination, a place where he thought he might be safe.

A place where he could set things right, too.

He had dipped into his memory files long enough to know that the place he wanted to get to was a considerable distance from here. Well beyond the city's limits. He'd do the trip on his paws if he had to, but it would take days, if not weeks. It would be better if he could travel in some kind of vehicle.

But a dog, even a dog as advanced as he, could not exactly rent a car and get behind the wheel, or even walk along the side of the highway and stick out his paw to hitch a ride. And while his software allowed him to think in ways that other dogs could not – by using actual words and language – he did not have the power of speech. He could not go up to someone and say, 'Can I get a lift?'

Imagine if he could. The sensation it would cause. Just as well he couldn't utter anything more than a bark. He'd be on the six o'clock news, or sold to a circus.

So even though he couldn't go up to the counter at the bus station and ask for a ticket, it didn't mean he couldn't get a *ride* on a bus. You just couldn't expect to get a seat. But maybe you could ride with the luggage.

He consulted his database, went into the map program, and found a location for a terminal that dispatched buses to places outside the city. It was only ten blocks away. At the next corner he made a left, then a right three blocks after that. Within fifteen minutes he was across the street from the bus station. He watched as the vehicles pulled in and out, diesel exhaust spewing from under the back bumpers. Even from across the street, the diesel fumes found their way into his nose. Chipper loved distinguishing between the thousands of smells the world presented him, but diesel exhaust was one he could do without.

He looked at the destinations over the front windshield. There was BUFFALO and PITTSBURGH and OTTAWA and NEW YORK and plenty of other places, but none of those cities was close to where he was going.

Chipper needed to see the schedule.

He darted across the street, narrowly avoiding getting run over by a taxi, its horn blaring, and dashed between a man's legs as he opened the heavy, brass-framed door to the terminal.

'Whoa!' the man said.

The dog trotted into the terminal, craning his head upwards, looking for a schedule. His eyes landed on it.

BOSTON, TORONTO, SYRACUSE, RICHMOND, MONTREAL—

He didn't want to go to any of those places. His eyes kept scanning the board.

PROVIDENCE, DAYTON, CANFIELD, CHIC—

Whoa! Hang on. There it was: CANFIELD.

That wasn't the *exact* place he wanted to go, but it was as close as any bus was going to take him. Once he got to Canfield, he could walk the rest of the way. His GPS program told him it was eight miles from Canfield to where he wanted to be.

That might take Chipper a day or so, but he could do it.

He checked to see what time the Canfield bus left and was alarmed to see that it was due to leave the station in the next five minutes. Which meant that it was probably already here, loading with passengers.

Chipper scurried back outside and ran to the platform where the buses lined up. He looked at the destination boards posted over the front windshields. The sign on the fourth bus read CANFIELD.

Chipper had to get on that bus.

Passengers were lined up, waiting to board. Most were already on, and seated. A man Chipper figured was the driver was midway down the side of the bus, directing passengers to leave their larger bags with him. As passengers boarded, the driver, the name YABLONSKY stitched to his uniform, opened a low, large, rectangular door beneath the windows and between the front and rear wheels. He began tossing the bags into the empty, cavernous storage area.

Chipper assessed the situation. The driver, while loading the bags, was keeping an eye on the people getting on the bus, which meant he was facing forward. Chipper slunk down the other side of the bus, came across the back, and peered his head around the corner. The driver, his back to him now, was still loading bags. But there were only a few to go.

Chipper had to get in there without being seen. And that meant timing it just right.

There was a sudden squealing sound. Chipper looked towards the street that ran past the terminal, saw two large, black SUVs with windows so darkly tinted he could not see who was inside.

The Institute.

Four men jumped out of each vehicle. But these were not the White Coats, not the men and women that Chipper had seen most days – the ones who poked and prodded him, who put devices inside him and took them out again, who sat at their computers and typed and clicked and printed out results. These men and women getting out of the SUVs were like the ones who'd been looking for him on the subway. Black suits, white shirts – ties on the men – little wires running down from their ears into their jackets.

They conferred briefly, pointed up and down the street, then in his direction. They were dividing up the search.

One of them headed towards the buses.

Chipper crouched down below the massive vehicle, inching forward so that he tucked behind the wheel, hidden from sight. He peeked around the edge, saw a man coming in his direction.

Did The Institute have people searching for him all over the city, or were they tracking him? Were the implants that allowed The Institute to know where he was at all times activated? There would have been no need to have that program engaged when they had him locked up in a cage.

The bus driver loaded the last of the bags. In seconds he'd be closing the door to the luggage compartment. Chipper crept around the tyre, his snout almost sticking out from under the vehicle.

The driver, who had been down on his knees pushing bags deeper into the cargo hold, stood. An arm went up.

This is it.

The broad, vertical metal door started to swing down. When it was halfway to closing, Chipper sprung out from under the bus and scooted into the cargo hold, unseen by the driver as he watched the passengers board. Chipper brought his hind legs in just as the door slammed shut, nearly closing on his still-sore tail.

It was completely dark inside the cargo compartment. Chipper, moving blindly, worked his way between and over the bags until he was near the back of the luggage hold. When the door next opened, he didn't want to be spotted. He snuggled down between some bags and rested his head on his outstretched paws.

Moments later, the bus engine began to grumble and Chipper could feel the huge, lumbering beast back slowly out of its spot, stop, then lurch forward.

I'm getting away. I'm getting away. It's going to be okay.

For a brief moment, Chipper felt encouraged. And then he coughed.

The smell of exhaust inside the cargo hold was strong.

He hoped he had enough air to last him till he got there.

08

Daggert was back in Madam Director's office with an update.

'I've pulled my team together and we're heading out.'

'Last I heard,' she said, 'the animal was cornered in the subway. I thought this was wrapped up.'

'No. They think now that he may have been hiding in a cello case when they went through the car. Then he got away.'

Madam Director, seated behind her desk, touched her fingers together, making her hands into a tent. Her nails were long and painted blood red.

'So where is the dog now?'

'Unknown. Another team converged on the bus station, but they could not find it.'

'Surely you didn't expect the beast to buy itself a ticket?'

'No.'

Madam Director's eyes narrowed. 'Perhaps you

should find out if the dog has bought a bicycle and is pedalling out of town.'

Daggert remained stone-faced as she asked, 'How did they know to look in the subway in the first place? And then the bus terminal?'

'Control managed to remotely activate the GPS locater, but it's not been working perfectly. They probably would have replaced the software in the animal if it hadn't been slated for termination.'

'You understand, Daggert, why we must get this animal back?'

Daggert nodded.

'Even if the animal attempted to pass itself off as a normal dog, and were to be taken in by some kind family, adopted as a stray, it would be found out as not being like other dogs. They'll find the port built into its collar. Perhaps they will, out of curiosity, try plugging in a laptop or some other device just to see what happens. Can you imagine that scenario, Daggert?'

'Yes. Although, as you know, there is the five-digit password protection.'

'Good heavens, is that the level of our sophistication? Is this dog as easy to get into as an ATM? What do you think will happen if someone gets into the program?'

'I expect they might call someone. Police, newspapers, the six o'clock news.'

'Yes. And we would risk becoming exposed. Our work would become public knowledge. A vital security program jeopardised. And once the world found out what we were doing with animals, imagine what else they might uncover? Reporters start digging, they might find out that the dogs are just the beginning of what we're working on here. We've faced a crisis like this before; a threat of exposure.'

'I know,' Daggert said. 'And as you will recall, I solved it.'

'Yes,' she said slowly. 'But it was very messy, Daggert. There was a lot of collateral damage.'

'I got the job done.'

'Well, now you have a new one,' Madam Director said in a clipped tone. She ran the fingers of one hand through her long, red hair. 'I'm worried about more than exposure. Suppose one of our enemies got hold of this mutt? Took him apart, figured out what made him tick? Can you imagine the damage?'

'It would be catastrophic.'

'That's why our most expedient solution may be to find this dog and destroy it. Recovering his internal workings intact would be nice, but keeping what we do here from going public is the priority.'

Daggert nodded. 'Understood. And if we are unable to maintain the GPS connection, we have another option.'

'Yes?'

'The optical feed.'

The woman cocked her head, reminding Daggert for a moment of the look he got from The Institute's dogs when they were puzzled. It was an observation he chose not to share with her.

'Video,' he said. 'The animal, as you know, is fitted with optical hardware that allows us to see what it sees. He is, essentially, a surveillance system with fur. If we can see what the dog sees, we can run it through landmark recognition. For example, if the dog were in Times Square, we'd recognise that pretty quickly, and could get there and find him.'

'We're not in New York, Daggert,' the Director said.

'As I said, that's an example. It doesn't have to be a major landmark. It can be anything you might be able to see on Whirl360, the site that allows you to see what's on any street in the world. But at the moment, the optical hardware, like the GPS system, is not operating at peak efficiency. I have Watson working on it.'

'Who's Watson?'

Daggert thought. He could never remember the man's name. 'Not Watson. *Wilkins.* He hopes to have a fix soon. Meanwhile, we've fanned out across the city. We're checking parks, in case the animal's more instinctive side comes into play and it wants to chase a few squirrels.'

Madam Director shook her head slowly and sighed. 'Get out,' she said. 'Get out and find that dog. Get down on your hands and knees and start sniffing other dogs' butts if you have to.'

09

Once the luggage compartment door was closed and the bus was in motion, Chipper attempted to get comfortable in spite of the unpleasant exhaust smell. He'd wedged himself in behind an oversized suitcase, and when he started to be troubled by an itch just behind his ear, he was unable to get his hind leg in position to scratch it.

So he backed out from behind the suitcase and found an area about three feet by three feet where there were no bags. He had to find this spot by moving around and bumping into things, because there was no light in here at all. He was working blind. Even though The Institute had equipped him with very special eyes that could transmit images and record video, he did not come with a set of headlights. What he needed right now was a miner's hat made for a dog.

When he found a spot he liked, he circled it twice the way dogs do, then lay down. And scratched. And scratched and scratched and scratched.

That felt better.

For the first time today, he had a moment to think. And as he so often did, he thought about the kind of dog he used to be.

A plain old pooch, that's what he once was.

He was one of a litter of six border collies born on a farm. It was a sheep farm, and Chipper's mother did what border collies did best. She rounded up those sheep at the end of every day, nipping at their heels, barking at them like a drill sergeant. Some of Chipper's earliest memories were of scampering after his mother in the field, his five brothers and sisters bouncing along with him.

What a wonderful time it was, growing up on the farm. But it did not last long.

One day, when Chipper was nearly a year old and still playful as a puppy but fully grown, a man and a woman arrived at the farm in a black car. Chipper didn't understand words back then, so he didn't know what they and the farm owner said to each other. But soon after the conversation, Chipper found himself in the back of the car, being driven away. He recalled leaping up in the back seat, paws on the rear window ledge, watching the farmhouse recede into the distance.

And his mother chasing after him, but finally having to give up when the car hit the main road and the woman behind the wheel hit the gas.

He was taken to a place where there was no grass or sheep or barns or fields or chickens or anything at all like that. What he remembered was a lot of white. White walls and white floors and white lights and men and women in white coats.

And then, everything went totally and completely black.

He did not know how long the blackness lasted. A week? A month? Maybe as much as a year? Of course, time meant nothing to him before the blackness. It was only after he emerged from the blackness that he began to be aware of time.

When he came out of the blackness, he was aware of much, *much* more than just time.

He was aware of *everything*.

They had done things to him. Put things into him. Taken out some parts of him that were real and replaced them with other parts that were not.

As a pup, he'd loved to be overwhelmed with the multitude of smells the world offered. Hundreds of scents wafted up his nostrils and he could very quickly distinguish one from another. It was like radar for the nose, and Chipper loved it. And he could handle it, too.

But when he awoke from the darkness, it wasn't just that they'd awakened his other senses – of touch, sight, hearing and taste. They had done that, to be sure, but it was as though Chipper had not just five finely attuned senses now, but five *million*.

Whenever there was something he wanted to know – the weather, the time, where he was, even something like 76,354 divided by 297 – he just knew it.

There were two White Coats who worked with him, eased him into his new life and new capabilities. They were so nice. They comforted him when he was frightened and overwhelmed. He no longer had a mother, but they were almost like parents to him.

He loved them.

And then, they were gone.

Chipper coughed.

He rested his snout on his forelegs and thought about where the bus was going. From the way it had been described to him long ago, his destination sounded like a wonderful place. Out in the country, on a lake. Far, far away from the city's loud noises and traffic and thousands of people.

Chipper coughed again.

The Institute had taken Chipper and the other animals out in the country a few times, and it was always his favourite part of training. It was like being a puppy again, back on the farm. A rainbow of scents. Flowers and grasses and earth and birds and pollen and squirrels – oh yes, *squirrels*! – plus rabbits and skunks and possums and chipmunks and snakes and frogs and wasps and ants and, well, the list went on and on.

It was so nice in the country. He hoped that where he was going would be like that.

Chipper coughed again. There was something seriously wrong with the air in this storage compartment. It was a sickening smell. Dirty and oily, and it seemed to be pushing away what little air was in here.

Diesel exhaust from the bus was leaking into the luggage area.

Chipper tried to hold his breath, but he was only able to do that for a few seconds. And when he went to breathe in again, he ended up taking even more of that noxious exhaust into his lungs.

Chipper now realised this wasn't the best place to hide after all. It was dawning on him that if he stayed in here much longer, he would die.

Cough cough cough.

He rose on all fours and started working his way over to the closed door. There were a lot of suitcases in his way, but there was about a foot of space between the top of the bags and the roof of the storage compartment. Chipper, his head and back rubbing up against the top of the hold, crawled awkwardly over them until he was up against the door.

He sniffed around, rubbed his nose up against the metal, looking for a button or a lever or anything that would make the door lift up, but found nothing. The only way to open it was on the outside, he figured.

More coughing.

Chipper's head throbbed. And even though, in total darkness, he had no visual sense of up or down or left and right, he was feeling dizzy.

The dog was losing consciousness.

He didn't know how long it would take for the bus to reach Canfield. A couple of hours, he figured, and he had been on the bus for the better part of an hour. He checked his built-in software: exactly seventy-two minutes to go. Could he last another hour?

Chipper did not believe he could.

He gave his head a shake and kept running his nose along the edge of the door. He managed to push one bag about six inches away from it, dropped his nose down, and saw a sliver of light at the bottom of the door, a crack to the outside.

Chipper pressed his nose up against the crack, getting whiffs of fresh air from outside.

He sniffed and sniffed and sniffed.

The dizziness held off slightly, but the headache was unrelenting. And the coughing wasn't letting up, either.

This tiny sliver of fresh air was only going to buy Chipper a bit of time, but it was not going to save him. He dared not move away from it, worried that as soon as he did, the exhaust fumes would overwhelm him.

Sniff sniff sniff.

The headache was getting worse. Chipper was starting to feel sleepy.

Sniff sniff.

He began to feel less concerned about his situation. He was starting to think maybe he didn't feel that bad after all.

He began to dream that he was back at the farm.

There was his mother, herding the sheep. Looking his way, encouraging him to follow. Chipper stumbling along after her on his short, puppy legs.

I'm coming, Mom! Wait for me!

What a lovely place to be. No worries, no cares. All you had to do was run around and play and chase the sheep.

Sni—

10

The next day, Jeff was standing on the end of the dock when a small aluminium boat, no bigger than his own twelve-footer, came speeding towards him from the east. The outboard bolted to the back was going full throttle, which brought the bow up and kept Jeff from seeing who was sitting in the back, driving it.

It got closer and closer without slowing down and Jeff feared the boat was going to crash into the dock.

He took a cautious step back.

A couple of seconds before it would have hit the dock, the boat veered sharply, throwing a large wave over the end and soaking Jeff's running shoes. That was when he saw that the person sitting in the back of the boat, one hand gripped to the outboard's throttle, was Emily Winslow. She was in white shorts and a red T-shirt, and on top of this, an orange life jacket.

'Hey!' Jeff shouted. 'You got my shoes wet!'

She didn't hear him over the sound of the motor,

and he couldn't hear her either, but he could see that she was laughing.

'Hey!' Jeff shouted again.

Emily spun the boat around sharply, and Jeff wondered if she was going to try to dowse him a second time, but before she reached the dock she cut the throttle back to a soft *put-put-put.*

'Look what you did to my shoes!' Jeff said.

She made a sad face. 'You live on a lake and you're afraid to get your shoes wet?'

'You drive like a maniac,' he told her.

'I've been driving this boat since I was five,' she said.

'You'd think by now you'd be good at it.'

She scowled at Jeff briefly, then asked, 'You wanna go for a ride?'

'With you?'

Her eyes rolled. 'No, with Captain Nemo. Of course, with me.'

Jeff glanced back towards the cottages, wondering whether Aunt Flo was spying on him. Just because he didn't see her didn't mean she wasn't lurking behind a tree.

He decided to risk it and said to Emily, 'Okay, but I can't be gone long. I've got like five acres of grass to cut.' At least Aunt Flo had a riding mower and he didn't have to do it all by hand.

'Then get in,' she said. 'But you have to put on the

life preserver thingy.' There was a second vest on the floor of the boat near the middle seat.

Jeff stepped in, slipping slightly as his wet soles met the metal hull, and threw on the life vest. The second he put his butt on the middle seat Emily twisted the throttle full blast. The boat shot forward, nearly knocking Jeff off his seat. He planted his wet shoes hard against the metal bottom to maintain his position. The metal vibrated on the choppy water as they skimmed across the surface of the lake. The way he was sitting, he was looking at where they'd been, but Emily had her eyes fixed forward, and she had those eyes on something.

Jeff lifted his legs and spun around on the bench-like seat so that he was looking the same way. They were headed towards a huge cabin cruiser that was leaving a large wake behind it.

'Hang on!' Emily said, aiming for the waves.

'What are you doing?' Jeff shouted, but Emily either couldn't hear him over the roar of the outboard, or wasn't interested in answering his question.

The tiny boat hit the first wave and it felt like they were in the air! Then there was a huge *WHOMP!* as the boat came back down on the water. Then there was another wave, and another *WHOMP!*

Jeff felt his butt lift off the seat, then drop back down. He reached out with both hands and gripped the edges – or gunnels – of the boat to keep his balance.

Emily shouted something he couldn't hear, so he turned around and said, 'What?'

She pointed. 'Here comes a huge one!'

By the time he'd turned around, they'd hit a third wave – and she was right. It was a doozy. Jeff's butt went a full six inches off the seat before it came back down hard.

'Ouch!' he cried.

He noticed that Emily had lifted her own butt off the seat just before they came down. She'd known what was coming and prepared for it, but hadn't bothered to tell Jeff.

'Sore butt?' she asked, and laughed without waiting for an answer.

She throttled back on the motor, which brought the bow down. She stood, still straddling her seat, reached for a handle on the back of the outboard and pulled hard, exposing the shaft and the propeller. Things had suddenly gone wonderfully quiet.

'Just checking to see if I picked up some weeds on the prop,' she said. 'Looks okay.'

Jeff noticed, off to his left about thirty feet away, a red buoy. Basically a metal post, about six to eight feet tall, which marked the route boaters should take through this part of the lake. Much further off was a similar buoy, but that one was black.

'What are we doing here?' he asked.

Emily, still standing, was looking into the water as they slowly glided along.

'I think I've had enough of hanging out with you,' she said. 'I'm out of here.'

And just like that, she stepped out of the boat as casually as if she were stepping out onto a dock.

But there was no dock.

'*Emily!*'

She went into the water, but Jeff couldn't believe what his eyes were seeing. There was a splash as she left the boat, but instead of her entire body plunging in, she was standing next to the boat, the water only up to her knees. She grabbed the boat with two hands to make sure it didn't drift away.

'So how's it going?' she asked.

Jeff's jaw dropped so far a seagull could have flown into his mouth and made a nest there.

'And you thought only Jesus could walk on water,' Emily said.

Jeff peered over the edge of the boat. About a foot down, he could see rocks.

'I don't get it,' he said. 'We're out in the middle of the lake.'

'I know!' she said. 'It's the coolest thing. So, years and years and years ago, this didn't used to be a lake. It was farmland. And then they put a dam in up around Canfield, and let this flood over and it became Pickerel Lake.'

'Whoa,' he said. 'So what are you standing on?'

'It's a wall,' she said. 'One of the farmers was separating his property from someone else's, so he made a wall with a huge pile of rocks, to act as a kind of fence.' She pointed – first at the red buoy, and then towards land. 'It starts over there, and then goes about halfway back to shore. It's about six feet wide. Come on, try it out. Your shoes are already wet. Just drop the anchor so we don't lose the boat.'

Jeff found the anchor – a sand-filled bleach bottle, just like Aunt Flo put in her boats – up front, tied off to the bow. He dropped it over the side onto the top of the wall, then put one leg over the side, and then the second.

Jeff was standing in the middle of the lake.

'This is totally cool,' he said.

Emily was kicking her legs up, like a dancer. '*La da la de da!*'

Jeff did the same. He started singing a song called 'One', from his mother's favourite musical, *A Chorus Line*. He'd never seen it, and had never wanted to see it. The idea of going to a musical was not his idea of a good time. But he loved to hear his mom belt it out in the kitchen. If his dad was there, he'd join in, link arms with her, and they'd kick up their legs in sync, like those whaddya-call-'em dancers, the Rockettes.

'Come here,' Jeff said, extending an arm. He slipped it over Emily's shoulder, and she hooked hers over his. When he kicked up his left leg, she kicked up her left. When he kicked up his right, she kicked up her right.

Anybody passing by wouldn't have believed it. Two people, practically standing on the water, kicking up their heels like a couple of Broadway stars.

It was pretty neat, except they hadn't noticed that with each kick, they'd gotten a little closer to the edge.

Jeff was the one who slipped first, and because he had his arm looped around Emily, she went in right after him. They both went in over their heads. They bobbed to the surface, spat out water, then clambered back onto the wall.

'Yuck,' Emily said. 'The rocks are all slimy.'

Once they were safely back on the wall, they climbed back into the boat.

'Well, that was fun until it wasn't,' she said. She looked at what a mess Jeff was and said, 'Man, your parents are going to kill me.'

'They're not going to kill you,' he said.

'Oh, yeah, you're spending the summer with your aunt, right? Your parents back in the city?'

Like a drenched dog, he gave himself a shake and wiped water out of his eyes. 'I don't have any parents,' he said.

Emily looked baffled. 'What? You mean, like, you were made in a test tube?'

'No, you idiot. They're *dead*.'

Her face fell and he immediately regretted calling her a name. 'I'm sorry,' he said.

'Me, too,' she said sombrely. 'Your mom *and* your dad?'

'Yup.'

'Like, did they get sick? I mean, did one get sick, and then the other get sick?'

'It wasn't like that.'

'I mean, I don't think I've ever met a kid whose parents were *both* dead,' Emily said. 'In case you're wondering why I have so many questions.'

'It's okay.'

'My mom died a few years ago,' she said. 'She had cancer. So it's just me and my dad now. If something happened to him I don't know what I would do.'

'My mom and dad died in a plane crash.'

Emily's eyes went wide. 'Are you kidding?'

'No. Why would a person kid about something like that? There'd have to be something wrong in your head to make a joke like that.'

'Yeah, I guess,' she agreed. 'So like, they were on a big jet and it crashed?'

He shook his head and held up a hand. 'Just stop talking and let me tell the story.'

She nodded, made a motion like she was zipping her lips shut.

'So, a year ago, my mom and dad were flying from New Jersey to Boston and—'

'Was this a vacation?'

'No, it was *not* a vacation. It was work.'

'Your mom and dad worked together?'

He glared at Emily.

'Sorry,' she said. 'Go on.'

'Okay, they worked for this drug company doing research into how to help people with allergies, and they were going from one meeting to another meeting and soon after the plane took off in New Jersey something went wrong with the plane.'

'Wowzer,' Emily said.

'So anyway, they were out over water. Long Island Sound. Something went wrong with the plane, and it blew up and went into the water, and my mom and my dad and the pilot and thirty-seven other people were all killed.'

'Whoa. That's awful. It blew up?'

'They think it was a wiring problem. Like, a short circuit or something, and that caused a spark, and then a fire started. So, now I live with my Aunt Flo. She had to take me in, although I don't think she really wanted to. But she's put me to work at her camp. She made me get rid of my dog.'

'What?'

'I had a dog, but she wouldn't let me live with her if I kept it because she hates dogs, so I had to get rid of it.'

'That sucks.'

'Yeah. Kinda a lot.'

'So you live here all the time now with your aunt?'

'Well, for a while I still lived in the city with some people who were friends of my parents, while things got wrapped up. Like my house getting sold and stuff like that. But these people didn't want to adopt me or anything, so my aunt said I could live with her if I helped her out, so here I am. And when I go to school in September, it'll be in Canfield.'

'Do you, like, know anyone there?'

Jeff shook his head. 'All my friends are back in the city. I don't have any friends up here.'

'That totally sucks,' Emily said.

Jeff suddenly felt very sad. 'I think you should take me back.'

Emily smiled. 'I'll drive around some more and so you'll be mostly dry when I drop you off. I promise not to jump any more big waves. Grab the anchor.'

Jeff pulled the anchor back into the boat while Emily used an oar to shove them away from the rock wall. She pushed the outboard motor back down so that the prop was again submerged.

But before she pulled the cord to bring it back to life, she looked at Jeff with sympathetic eyes and said, 'You want to see something else that's cool?'

'Like what?'

'Something I've never shown anybody before,' she said.

'What?'

'My hideaway,' she said. 'A train station in the forest.'

'A train station in the forest? That doesn't make any sense.'

She smiled. 'That's what makes it so cool.'

'Okay, folks, if you can just wait a minute I'll have all these bags out of here!'

The bus's cargo-bay door had swung open, filling the compartment with light. Yablonsky, the driver, immediately began grabbing bags and setting them onto the tarmac.

'Just have a look for your bag and take it,' he said, crouching down, grabbing at handles, dragging the bags out. 'Oh, my back,' he said under his breath.

Then: 'Holy mackerel, what's this?'

A couple of the passengers grabbing their luggage leaned over to peer into the cargo bay.

'It's a dog!' one yelled.

'It's dead!' said another.

'Oh, no!' said Yablonsky, who pushed bags out of the way so he could crawl into the bay on his knees.

Chipper lay on his side, eyes closed, not moving.

'Hey, fella, come on now, you okay?' said the driver, reaching a hand out to tentatively touch the dog's fur.

He stroked his side a couple of times. 'How'd you get in here? How'd you get in here, boy?'

'Is he dead?' a woman asked.

'I don't know,' Yablonsky said, worriedly. He rested his hand on the dog's side. Did the dog's chest cavity move? He wasn't sure. But one thing he *was* sure of: if this dog was breathing, he wasn't breathing very hard. He crouched down, got his arms under Chipper, carefully moved him out of the cargo area and set him gently onto the pavement.

'Oh, no!' several passengers said in unison. One shouted, 'Someone needs to do something! Call an ambulance!'

'An ambulance?' said another passenger. 'For a dog?'

'The fire department,' said someone else, getting out a cell phone and starting to tap some buttons. 'They help dogs and cats!'

'No time,' said the driver quietly to no one in particular. 'I'll have to do it myself.'

'Do what?' someone asked.

'Mouth to mouth,' Yablonsky said.

'*What?*' said several of his passengers.

What they did not know was that their bus driver loved dogs very much, had three at home, and he knew it was possible to save a dog the way you would a person who had stopped breathing. The first thing he did was open Chipper's mouth and stick his fingers in to make sure nothing was blocking the animal's windpipe. Finding nothing there, he lifted up the dog's head, put one hand around his snout to keep his mouth mostly closed, then put his own mouth over the dog's mouth and nose and blew as hard as he could.

'Ewww,' said a passenger.

But most of the passengers weren't making a sound, except for one who was briefly on the phone to call for help, and no one was grabbing a bag and walking away. They were fascinated by what was happening before them.

Yablonsky blew hard into the dog's snout, took his own mouth away to take in a deep breath of his own, then repeated the process.

Someone snapped a picture. 'I'm posting this for sure!' a woman said.

The driver didn't want his picture taken, but he was more concerned with saving the dog than telling the woman to stop it.

Breath after breath after breath.

'Come on,' he whispered pleadingly to the dog, while taking in another deep breath.

And then, suddenly, Chipper's eyes opened. He gave his head a shake, forcing the driver to stop the lifesaving exercise.

The dog's chest could be seen going up and down.

'You did it! You saved him!' the passengers shouted.

'You need mouthwash!' another yelled.

Chipper took in several more breaths on his own and surveyed the scene in front of him. All these people standing around, looking at him, cheering and clapping. And there was this man in a uniform on the ground with him. Chipper remembered him from when he'd first hidden on the bus.

He saved my life.

Chipper observed several people on phones.

Oh, no, he thought. *That's not good.*

If someone had called the police, they'd probably take him to a veterinary hospital.

Put him in a cage. Try to find his owner.

Chipper didn't have an owner. Chipper had had a *captor*. He did not want to be returned to The Institute.

With great effort, Chipper got to his feet. He raised himself up on his front two paws, then pushed his back end up with his hind legs. He wobbled slightly.

'You take it easy there, fella,' said Yablonsky. 'You were nearly a goner.'

Chipper struggled to access files, the GPS program in particular. Where were they? Where had the bus stopped? Was this Canfield?

'I'm gonna take you home,' said the driver. 'Help you get your strength back, then find out who you belong to. Let me have a look at your collar there.'

Before Chipper could pull away, the man had grabbed hold of him by the band that went around his neck.

'What the—' He was struggling to get his fingers between the collar and the dog, but could not. 'This collar, it sure is tight . . . no, wait a second. Is this thing . . . it's like it's stitched right to you.'

Chipper, still waiting for coordinates to load so he'd know where he was, pulled away from the man in one, sudden jerk.

He heard something. Off in the distance. His ears perked up.

A siren.

Someone was coming. Police, maybe the fire department.

Chipper spun around and ran, disappearing under the bus.

'Hey!' the driver shouted. 'Come back here!'

The dog emerged out the other side. He figured the best thing was to run, for now. Find someplace to hide until he could recover, get his strength back.

No, wait.

There was something else Chipper had to do first.

He stopped abruptly, turned around, and ran back towards the bus. Shot under it and came out the other side, where the driver was still kneeling, shaking his head in disbelief at Chipper's sudden disappearance.

The dog pounced on him, threw his paws onto the man's shoulders, and gave his face a huge, long lick of gratitude.

And then Chipper hopped back down and disappeared, once again, beneath the bus.

12

Daggert was in The Institute's main control room, where three men and three women were seated at a bank of computers. All wore headsets. Some monitors displayed maps, others lines of data.

'Come on, people, I need something, anything!'

Everyone continued clicking and tapping.

'Why can we not get the tracker activated?' Daggert asked of everyone.

A man raised his hand. 'Working on that, sir.'

'Watson?' Daggert said, moving to the man's work station.

'Wilkins,' he said. 'Trying to reboot remotely is presenting some problems. For a while there, when I thought I was almost about to lock on, I lost the signal. It was almost like the animal had gone into a steel cage or something.'

'A steel cage?' Daggert said. 'What do you mean, a steel cage? What kind of cage?'

'Not a cage, necessarily. But some kind of

enclosure with metal walls that inhibited the signal. I totally lost him, and now I'm having to try again from scratch.'

'Well stop wasting time talking to me then, and do it!'

'Yes, sir, of course. I was only—'

From across the room, a woman removed her headset and shouted, 'I've got something!'

All eyes turned on her.

'What is it?' Daggert demanded.

'Some emergency chatter,' she said. 'Someone made a call to nine-one-one.'

Daggert knew The Institute's sophisticated equipment could listen in on police, fire and ambulance transmissions. They could even intercept cell phone calls. They had instructed their surveillance program to listen for key words. Today, there was only one word they had their ears open for.

Dog.

'What was the call about?' Daggert demanded.

'Hang on,' she said. 'I'm pulling it up on my screen.'

She tapped a few buttons until what looked like a small set of controls appeared on her screen across the bottom: buttons for play, stop, fast forward, reverse. 'What you're going to hear is an emergency operator, and a woman calling in.' She clicked on play.

Squiggly lines, representing voices, began to move across the screen.

OPERATOR: How may I direct your call?

WOMAN: The dog isn't breathing!

OPERATOR: A dog, ma'am?

WOMAN: (*bringing her voice down to a whisper*) The bus driver's giving him mouth-to-mouth right now! I've never seen anything like it.

OPERATOR: What is your location?

WOMAN: The bus station.

OPERATOR: Which bus station?

WOMAN: Canfield!

OPERATOR: And what exactly happened?

WOMAN: This dog somehow got trapped in the place under the bus where the luggage goes? And when the driver opened it up, the dog looked like it was dead.

OPERATOR: And the driver's trying to revive him now?

WOMAN: That's right!

OPERATOR: I'll dispatch someone right away.

The clip ended.

Daggert said, 'That would explain it. The steel cage. The dog was in that cargo hold.' He smiled. He entered a number into the cell phone already in his hand, put the phone to his ear.

'Bailey?' he said. 'Get Crawford and bring the car around.'

The woman who'd intercepted the emergency call had her headset back on, and was waving her hand in the air. Daggert approached.

'What?'

'They've arrived on the scene,' she said.

'Yes?'

'The dog's gone.'

Daggert's teeth ground together. 'Find me that bus driver.'

13

'This is awesome!' Jeff said. 'Unbelievable!'

When Emily led him into the acres of woods between Flo's Cabins and Shady Acres Resort, he really wasn't expecting to see a train station. He thought she had to be telling him a crazy story.

But there it was.

Emily's secret fort really was a *train station*. In the middle of the forest.

It was missing, however, the single most important ingredient for any successful train station.

Tracks.

There were none. Not only that, there was no platform where the passengers would have waited. The building was propped up on concrete blocks, so you could see right under it.

In addition to no tracks and no platform, there were no boxcars, no passenger cars, not one caboose and not a single engine.

But of all the things that were not here, it was the

absence of tracks that puzzled Jeff the most. There wasn't even a straight pathway through the forest where tracks might have once been.

'Pretty cool, huh?' Emily said.

The station was about twenty by forty feet, built of wood, and had small dormer windows poking out of the sloped, shingled roof. Hanging from below the eaves at one end was a sign that said CANFIELD, the name of the closest town.

'Where did the tracks go?' Jeff asked.

'There never were any.'

'Why does somebody build a train station where there are no train tracks?'

'They didn't. It got moved here,' she said. She pointed to an opening in the trees. There was a road, little more than two ruts, heavily overgrown with grass. 'They brought it in from the main road that way. The station used to be in town, but years ago they stopped passenger service and ripped up the tracks, so this rich guy bought it and had it moved into the woods here so he could make it into a cottage. But then he died, and the place has just sat here for years.'

'Doesn't anybody know about it?'

Emily shook her head. 'Nope. I mean, almost nobody. I found it when I was hiking. I asked my dad about it, and he told me about its history, but hardly anybody comes around here. It's my own special place. Come on, let's go inside.'

Several concrete blocks had been arranged into three steps that led up to the main door. Emily gave it a strong push – it was sitting crooked in the frame, which made sense, since the whole building was listing slightly to one side on the blocks – then took one huge final step to get inside.

Jeff followed her.

'Wow,' he said. 'This is very cool.'

The old wooden benches where passengers sat and waited for their trains were still there. So were the ticket windows, and printed schedules on the walls. But the place was a mess! The wallpaper was peeling, there were holes in the walls, bulbs in the lamps shattered. Old, yellowed newspapers were scattered across the floor, and there were marks in the ceiling where rain had seeped through.

'It's in pretty bad shape,' Emily conceded. 'The animals have gotten into it over the years. Birds have made nests, and—'

'*Holy crap!*' Jeff shouted.

Something had run over his foot.

'It's just a squirrel,' Emily said. 'You're a real outdoors person, aren't you?'

Jeff turned red with embarrassment. 'I just didn't see it.'

'And you kind of have to watch your step, because the floor is rotting in places. Like, when we go to the second floor, watch the steps. Some of them are pretty weak.'

She led him up a narrow stairwell, pointing along the way. 'Don't step on that one, or that one.'

Jeff was careful to follow in her exact footsteps.

The upstairs was only a fraction of the size of the first floor. The wall, following the rooflines, angled down, so a person could only stand upright in the middle of the room. There was still plenty of ripped wallpaper and stains in the ceiling, but there was one new thing, too. A big, cushy beanbag chair in the middle of the room. On the floor next to it, a stack of books and magazines and a deck of playing cards.

'This is my special place,' Emily said. 'Where I come to get away.'

'Get away from what?'

Emily sighed. Jeff was clearly exhausting her. 'Don't you ever just want to go someplace where no one can find you? So you can think, or read, or just do absolutely nothing?'

'I guess,' he said. 'Living with Aunt Flo, I feel that way every single day.'

'Right!' she said. 'This is that place for me.' She plopped herself down into the beanbag. 'This is my spot.'

'I'll be careful not to sit there,' he said.

'We could look for another chair, and that could be yours.'

Jeff liked that idea. 'Okay.'

He reached into his pocket for his cell phone to see what time it was. 'I really, really have to get back. Aunt Flo is going to be looking for me.'

'Well, she'd never find you here,' Emily said.

He grinned. He liked the idea of a place where Aunt Flo couldn't find him. He just wished there was a place he could go and find his parents.

14

Yablonsky was reading the *Canfield Examiner* and having a cup of coffee in the bus company's kitchen area when a woman poked her head in and said, 'Gus, there's some people here to see you.'

The driver put down the paper. 'TV people?'

He figured that video one of his passengers posted of him saving the dog's life would eventually draw the attention of the media. He wasn't hoping for it. Just expecting it. He didn't want any attention for breathing life into that mutt. His only regret was that the dog hadn't hung around so that he could try to locate its owner.

'I don't know,' the woman said. 'They don't look like TV people, but—'

Three people pushed past her and entered the room, the lead person flanked by another man and woman. Everyone dressed in black. The men were in suits, and woman in black slacks, blouse and jacket.

'You Gus Yablonsky?' the man in the middle asked.

Gus took another sip of his coffee. 'Who wants to know?'

'I'm Daggert,' he said.

'And these two?'

The woman said, 'I'm Bailey.' She pointed a thumb at the other man. 'This is Crawford.'

'Mr Daggert, Ms Bailey, Mr Crawford – I am pleased to make your acquaintance. I am, as you surmised, Gus Yablonsky.'

'We want to know about the dog.'

Gus tipped his head to one side, sized up his visitors. 'Where are the cameras? Aren't you from the TV station?'

'We're not from the TV station,' Daggert said. 'We want to know your involvement with the dog.'

'Involvement?'

'You enabled its escape.'

'Escape?' Gus shook his head and stood up. 'Look, Mr Daggert, I found the mutt in the cargo hold. He was nearly dead. I got him breathing again and he took off. End of story.'

Daggert's eyes narrowed. 'Why didn't you hold onto him?'

'I wanted to. But he got away.'

'Did someone take him from you?'

Gus blinked. 'Huh?'

'Was it all worked out ahead of time?' Daggert asked. 'Did you tell someone you'd be bringing the dog to the station? Was someone waiting for you and the dog to arrive?'

Gus said, again, 'Huh?'

'Are you really this stupid, Mr Yablonsky, or is someone paying you to act dumb?'

'Mister, have you been smoking something funny? Because you're not making any sense at all.'

Daggert gave a nod to Bailey and Crawford. They closed in on Yablonsky, grabbed him under the arms, dragged him across the room and pinned him against the wall.

Bailey produced a device in her free hand. Not a gun, but something with what looked like pincers on the end. She pressed a button, and a bolt of electricity crackled between the two points. A stun gun.

'Close the door, Crawford,' Daggert said.

'Whoa!' said Gus. 'Hang on!'

Daggert approached, his face an inch away from the bus driver's. 'I'm going to ask you again: Who you are working for? If I don't believe you, Bailey here will turn you into a light bulb. Now, who do you work for?'

'The Simpson Bus Company! I've worked here twenty-three years!'

Daggert pursed his lips, nodded at the woman. She released her grip on Yablonsky, hit a button on the weapon, and touched it to the man's stomach. It made a sound like a bug wandering into a zapper.

'Aggghhhh!' he shouted.

The man slid down the wall and crumpled onto the floor.

'One more time,' Daggert said. 'Who do you really work for?'

'I'm telling you the truth! The Simpson Bus Company!'

Daggert looked deeply into the man's eyes. 'You know what? I think I believe you.'

'It's true! It's true!'

'Do you know where the dog went?'

'He just ran away! Well, he came back just for a second.'

'He came back? Why?'

'To lick me,' Gus said.

'To lick you?'

'He wanted to thank me.'

Daggert considered that bit of information for a moment. 'Interesting,' he said. 'Did the dog try to communicate with you in any other way?'

'Communicate?'

Daggert sighed impatiently. 'Yes, *communicate*. Do you not understand me?'

'Like I said, he licked me. Is *that* communicating?'

'Nothing else?'

Now it was Gus who was becoming exasperated. 'Like *what*?'

Daggert shrugged. 'A series of eye blinks or tapping of paws, for example? Did he show you his port so that

107

you could link with him? Did the dog in any way attempt to speak to you?'

Gus, eyes wide with disbelief, said, 'Seriously, what have you been smoking?'

Daggert let out a long breath. 'He knows nothing,' he said to Bailey and Crawford. To Bailey, he said, 'Give it to him one more time, but set it to amnesia.'

Before Bailey zapped him again, she said, 'You're gonna lose an hour, you'll never know we were even here. You'll have one hell of a headache, but at least you'll be alive.'

'Who are you people?' Gus Yablonsky asked. 'Who do you work for? Who asks if a dog has communicated with them?'

Bailey smiled before she touched the stun gun to the bus driver's arm. His eyes rolled up into his head and he slid down to the floor.

15

When he'd first escaped The Institute, all Chipper had worried about was getting away. But now that he was many miles away, and off that bus – *Oh, that wonderful driver!* – the dog could assess his next step with more deliberation.

That meant getting his bearings.

He had made it to Canfield, which was good. Not only was it the only place he wanted to go to, he felt it was the place he *had* to go. Once he'd fled the bus station, gotten outside the small town of Canfield and into the shelter of a wooded area, Chipper stopped. He needed to rest and give his lungs a chance to recover from being filled with exhaust.

It didn't matter how much technology the White Coats had built into him, Chipper still needed good old air to survive.

He settled into the leafy, forest floor, resting his head on his paws. Almost immediately, he spotted a squirrel running down one tree, across the ground, and up another.

Chipper could not be bothered to give chase. That's how tired he was.

But the squirrel sighting reminded Chipper that it had been a long time since he'd had anything to eat. Or drink. A squirrel might make a tasty snack, but he wasn't sure he had the strength or the speed to catch one.

Chipper's long jaw widened in a yawn. He eased his body onto its side into a pile of leaves and allowed himself to go to sleep.

And sleep he did. Right through the night.

He woke twice to almost total darkness. Not the kind of pitch-black darkness he'd experienced in the bus luggage compartment, where he couldn't see anything at all. This darkness was filled with gentle light. The star-filled night sky allowed him to take in his surroundings. He heard crickets, the scurrying of mice, an owl's hoot.

The sounds did not frighten Chipper. They comforted him. They were more reassuring than the sounds of The Institute. The laboured breathing of his fellow captives. The soft whir of the air conditioning. The tap-tap-tapping of computer keyboards.

It was neither sunlight nor sounds that woke him the next day.

It was the smell of something delicious.

Chipper opened his eyes, consulted his implanted clock. It was 11.09 a.m. He put his snout into the air, tracked the direction from which the smell had come.

East.

With some effort, he stood. He still did not feel right. Wobbly. That exhaust had really done a number on him.

But he was hungry. He put one paw in front of the other and followed the scent. It led him out of the woods to the back yards of a string of houses in a subdivision outside Canfield. Chipper saw swing sets and sandboxes and gardens. One yard, with a pool, was fenced off. The folks in the house next to it had a small plastic one, about four feet wide, that held barely a foot of water. Only a low hedge separated their garden from the woods.

A great place to get a drink.

But that yard offered something even better.

A barbecue. The lid was open, and Chipper could see something on the grill, sizzling.

A man emerged from a sliding glass door and walked over to the grill and flipped over whatever was on it. Then he went back into the house.

That was when Chipper made his move.

Swiftly, he emerged from the woods and vaulted the hedge. The first thing he had to do was quench his thirst, and the kiddie pool was like the biggest dog's bowl in the world. Chipper dropped his snout into it and furiously lapped up water.

His plan had been to check out the barbecue next, but when he heard the glass door slide open, he crouched low behind the pool. The man was back with an empty plate in his hand. With a set of tongs, he took three hot dog wieners from the grill and put them on the plate.

He put the plate on the shelf next to the barbecue, went back into the house and shouted, 'Where are the buns?'

Chipper went into action.

He came out from his hiding spot behind the pool, rose up on his hind legs, turned his snout sideways and snatched two of the three wieners from the plate. He dropped back down to all fours and ran.

The door opened again.

'Hey! Hey! Come back here!'

Chipper did not go back.

* * *

The wieners were delicious. Chipper was thinking they might just be the most delicious things he had ever eaten.

He sought shelter in the woods again before enjoying his takeout meal. He was careful to chew the wieners well so there was no risk of one of them getting caught in his throat. The meal was enough to make Chipper forget, at least for a few moments, all that he had been through.

He was *happy*.

And wasn't that exactly why the White Coats wanted to put him down? To end his life? He wasn't supposed to feel happy. He wasn't supposed to feel sad. He wasn't supposed to feel *anything*.

He was just supposed to do his job.

And where would he have performed this job, if he had turned out the way they'd wanted him to? Where would they have sent him? China? Russia? Afghanistan? Maybe someplace right here at home where they suspected some kind of nefarious activity going on? Someplace where a dog could hang around unnoticed, pick up things, overhear things, in a way no human being could?

Better to think about moving on.

So once he'd downed the wieners, he proceeded further into the forest. If his GPS program was to be trusted – and he had no reason to think it shouldn't be – sooner or later he would come out onto a road. If he followed it west, it would take him where he wanted to be.

He definitely had more of a spring in his step now. He moved confidently through the forest. Walking for a while, then running. Enjoying the thousands of different scents. Trees, flowers, animals, bugs, the earth beneath his paws.

There was a slight wind coming from the west, and with it came a variety of different smells. Rotting food. He could smell fish and vegetables and meat and all kinds of other things. Even some smoke, which suggested that some of these things were being burned. These were the types of smells a person would find pretty disgusting, but for Chipper it made the atmosphere all that much richer.

More stinky stuff! Love it!

He was tempted to go see where the smells were coming from, but he'd already lost enough time recovering from the bus incident, sleeping and finding food. And besides, he was nearly at the road.

Chipper emerged from the woods, stopped, looked left and then right. He'd come upon a gravel road. With the exception of an approaching pickup truck in the distance, trailing dust in its wake, there was no traffic.

The dog came up to the shoulder of the road, intending to trot along in a westerly direction.

Behind him, the truck got closer.

Chipper was beginning to feel . . . excited. He was almost at his destination. He wasn't sure what he'd do when he got there, but he'd play things as they came. He'd been doing that all day and it had been working out pretty well for him.

He couldn't wait to— *AHHHHH!*

There was suddenly an awful buzzing in Chipper's brain. Not his real brain, not the one he was born with, but something was going on with one of his attachments. An unbearable, internal screeching. It was akin to having a food processor whirring between one's ears on the highest setting.

He knew what was going on.

It was the White Coats.

They were trying to lock in on him. They were trying to initiate a reconnection.

He felt as though his head would explode.

And as the screeching continued, Chipper began to stumble. He became disoriented. His four legs had stopped working the way they were supposed to. He took a couple of sideways steps, then one forward, then one back.

What his eyes allowed him to see became distorted. The world turned upside down, then righted itself, then went sideways.

Chipper stumbled further into the middle of the road.

A horn blared.

Brakes squealed.

He was so close.

16

Aunt Flo was furious when Jeff got back to the camp.

'Where have you been?' she demanded to know when he came through the door of her house.

'Just out,' he said. 'I wasn't gone all that long.'

'Really? *Really?*' She'd made her hands into fists and had them jabbed into her hips, elbows out. It was her favourite stance. She was leaning against the kitchen counter in front of the sink. A lock of hair had slipped free of one of her bobby pins and was hanging across one eye. 'I want you to come with me,' she said.

Aunt Flo went to grab for Jeff's arm but he headed for the door too quickly for her. If there was something she wanted him to see, fine, but he wasn't going to let her physically drag him to it.

'This way!' she said. 'If you hadn't been goofing off, you'd have known what was going on here.'

She led him to the roofless enclosure where all the cans of garbage were kept, and filled, before they were taken to the dump. She opened the slatted wood door and said, 'Behold.'

Oh, wow.

Three of the trash cans had been tipped over, the lids removed, and the green bags dragged out and torn open. Food scraps and dirty napkins and all sorts of other disgusting things were spread across the ground.

'Uh oh,' Jeff said.

'Uh oh, indeed,' Aunt Flo said. 'Looks like *somebody* forgot to snap the lids on tight. You've turned this into a raccoon restaurant.'

Jeff had to admit it was possible. The raccoons around here were pretty smart, no doubt about that. They were like safecrackers when it came to getting into garbage cans.

'Looks like you've got your work cut out for you,' Aunt Flo said, then turned around and walked back to the house.

There were a lot of disgusting things in the world, but few were as disgusting as the guts of a garbage bag. As Jeff got closer he could see chicken bones and fish heads and coffee grounds and something oozy leaking out of one of the torn bags that looked like it could be blood from some kind of alien.

Jeff thought he might puke.

But somehow he kept the contents of his stomach in place while he shovelled all the mess into brand new trash bags. Then he went and got Aunt Flo's old pickup truck so that he could load everything into the back.

And then he was off to the dump.

Even though he'd already made dozens of trips down this road without any problems, Jeff still worried that one of these days he would be stopped by the police and arrested for driving without a licence. He thought Aunt Flo didn't worry about his being arrested mainly because it wouldn't be happening to her.

Jeff remembered what his father used to say about his older sister, Flo. How when they were growing up, she was always talking him into doing things she considered too risky to tackle herself. If her kite were stuck in a tree, she'd send her little brother up the trunk to retrieve it. Same thing when her Frisbee landed on the roof. Once, she talked him into stealing a bag of Fritos from the corner store when she was consumed with a junk food craving, and had no money.

So during the drive to the dump, Jeff kept glancing into the rear-view mirror, expecting to see a flashing red light accompanied by the whoop of a siren. He wondered whether some jail time wouldn't be just the rest he needed. Sitting behind bars might be a heck of a lot nicer than living under Aunt Flo's roof.

At least for a while.

The truck rumbled along the gravel road to the dump, dust stirring up behind it. Jeff fiddled with the radio – the truck was so old that there were actual push buttons for the individual stations – in a vain attempt to find something good to listen to. None of the buttons had been set to anything he liked – Aunt Flo was a country and western fan – so he had to turn the knob manually to find anything someone under a hundred might listen to.

Between glancing at the radio and checking his mirror for the police, Jeff didn't have his eyes on the actual road as much as he should.

He had just landed on a station playing something with a really good beat to it and was tapping his fingers on the top of the steering wheel when he saw something suddenly dart in front of the truck.

It had come out of the tall grasses on the right shoulder. Something black, with some white in it.

He thumped the horn as he moved his foot from the gas to the brake. He'd slammed it so hard he thought he'd snap the pedal off. The truck skidded to a halt on the gravel, back end fishtailing, the dust trail enveloping the vehicle and wafting in through the windows. Jeff coughed a couple of times as he waved away the dust in front of his face.

He had no idea what he'd hit, or if he'd actually hit anything at all. But that combination of black and white fur had given him a start. What if he'd run over a skunk? What if it was about to unleash the biggest fart the Canfield area had ever smelled? If Aunt Flo thought the garbage was a stinky mess, just wait till he brought her truck back reeking of skunk juice.

But no, what he'd seen was not a skunk. He'd seen it only for a fraction of a second, but it was way too big to be a skunk.

Jeff was going to have to screw up his courage and check out what it was.

He opened the door, stepped out of the truck, and came around the front very slowly.

His heart sank.

It was a dog.

Not just any dog, but a dog that looked a lot like Pepper. It wasn't Pepper – he could tell that right away from the black and white markings, but it was the same kind of dog.

A border collie, mostly black, with a bit of white fur on his snout and under his neck and on his legs. Or hers. He didn't know if it was a he or a she.

'Oh man, I'm so sorry!' he said to the dog.

The dog was lying on his side, and Jeff thought maybe he was dead because his eyes were closed, but then he saw his chest pump up and down. He was still breathing!

Jeff knelt down and gently lay his hand on his side. 'It's going to be okay,' he said. 'You're going to be all right!'

Of course, Jeff knew no such thing, but what else was he going to say? He continued moving his hand over him, tentatively checking to see whether anything was broken. There was no blood, and nothing about the dog looked bent out of shape. Jeff looked at the bumper of the pickup, and while there was no blood, there was a tiny wisp of black fur stuck to it. So the truck must have hit him, but maybe it had been nothing more than a nudge, not a serious blow. Jeff had hit those brakes fast and hard.

Jeff got his face right up next to the dog's, but struggled to focus as he found himself blinking away tears.

'Please don't die,' Jeff said as a tear rolled down his cheek. 'Please be okay.'

The dog's chest continued to go up and down, but other than that there was no sign of life.

Jeff started crying harder. This dog reminded him so much of Pepper. The dog he'd loved with all his heart that had been taken away from him, and if that weren't bad enough, now it looked like maybe he was going to be a dog murderer.

A tear dropped from his cheek and landed on the dog's black nose.

And it twitched.

'Hey,' Jeff said, and sniffed.

The nose twitched some more. Jeff stroked the dog's side soothingly.

And then, one eye fluttered open.

'Yes!' Jeff said. 'You're alive! You got hit. You ran across the road and I almost ran you right over. I hit the brakes. I hit 'em fast as I could. But you can't run into the road like that!'

The open eye blinked.

'Does anything hurt? Did anything get broke? Huh? Whose dog are you, anyway?'

Jeff felt around under the dog's jaw, looking for tags. He found a collar under the fur, but no tags.

'I'm going to try and lift you up, okay?' Jeff said. 'You shout out if it starts to hurt.'

Jeff slipped his arms under the dog and ever so slowly lifted him off the gravel. If anything hurt, he wasn't showing it. He was limp in the boy's arms.

'Gonna take care of you,' Jeff said. 'I'm going to make sure you're okay. And I'll find your owner. We're going to make it okay.'

Jeff came around the passenger side of the truck, managed to open the door, and carefully set the dog on the passenger seat.

The dog made a small whimpering sound as Jeff slipped his arms out from under him.

'You're going to be okay. I promise.'

Jeff closed the door and ran around to the other side of the truck. He had to take this dog someplace where he could look after him, but he couldn't take him home. Aunt Flo *hated* dogs.

At that moment, Jeff thought of Emily's train station. That was perfect! He would take the dog there.

'I know where I can take you,' Jeff said. 'I know a safe place.'

17

Daggert's cell phone rang.

'What?' he said. After leaving the bus station and hunting around Canfield for the dog, he, Bailey and Crawford had spent the night in a cheap motel. Now they were up, sitting in a diner, plotting their next step over a second cup of coffee.

'It's Wilkins, sir,' a man said.

'Wilkins? Who the hell are you?'

'I work in the control room, sir. I've worked for you for four years.'

'Oh yes, Watson. What is it you want?'

'I have good news and bad news.'

Daggert gritted his teeth. 'Bad news first.'

'We lost contact with the target. We'd almost re-established it, but then it was gone. We think there was some kind of impact, that the animal may have had a serious fall, or even been hit by something.'

'Hit by what?'

'Don't know. But it was enough to disrupt the circuitry, at least momentarily.'

'And you have good news?'

'Yes. Just before we lost our connection, we were able to pinpoint a more tentative location.'

'Yes?'

'The dog is near Canfield.'

'I already knew that, Watkins.'

'Wilkins, sir.'

'The dog got off a bus in Canfield. We're still in Canfield. Tell me something I don't already know.'

'We narrowed the dog's location to be west of the town. We did a GPS overlay and it was in the vicinity of the local garbage dump.'

'The dump?'

'Yes, sir. It's not far from where you are now.'

Daggert thought about that. It made sense. A dump would be a good place for the animal to hide out, and scrounge some food. Plus, there'd be rats. A magnificent buffet, if you were a dog.

'Send me that location,' Daggert said.

'Yes, s—'

Daggert ended the call. 'Leave your coffee,' he said to the other two. 'We're going to the dump.'

18

Jeff remembered that when Emily first showed him the train station, she'd pointed to a narrow, overgrown road that led in from the main one that went to Canfield. He trolled slowly along that route, and when he was roughly between the turnoff to Flo's Cabins and Shady Acres Resort, he kept his eye out for a possible way in.

Before long, Jeff noticed a rusted gate hanging between two wood posts and pulled off to the side of the road.

Jeff said to the dog, 'You wait here. I'm just going to check something.'

Chipper moved his head slightly at the sound of the boy's voice. He found comfort in it. He'd been watching him closely as he lay on the seat next to him. He saw features he recognised in the boy's face. The way his nose turned up slightly at the end. His blue eyes. Something about the way he held his head.

Yes, this is the one, Chipper thought. He hadn't

wanted to get hit by his pickup truck, but it had saved him a lot of time tracking him down.

Jeff leapt out of the truck and walked across the gravel shoulder to the gate. A length of chain had been looped around a hook to hold it in place, but there was no lock. He unwound the chain to free the gate and pushed it back, which wasn't easy, since it had to be forced over grass that had grown two feet high. And the rusted hinges didn't help much, either. This gate hadn't been opened in years, that was pretty clear.

Jeff got back in the truck, drove down the lane far enough to clear the gate, then went back and closed it, hooking it back up the way he'd found it.

Chipper sat up far enough in the seat to watch him do all this. He wanted to find a way to talk to him, explain things to him, but there wasn't any way he could do that right now. He'd have to give that some thought.

Jeff took the road very slowly. The tall trees on either side more or less defined it, but it didn't look like anyone had been down here in years. Parts of the road had washed out, exposing large rocks. It must have been quite a trick, years ago, getting that train station down here. It would have to have been on a flatbed truck, and taken off with a large crane. There had to have been enough room to get all that equipment down here at one time, but in the intervening years the forest had nearly reclaimed this road. And Jeff was guessing the road itself had been in a lot better shape back then. It was a good thing he was in a truck with lots of clearance; otherwise the undercarriage would have bottomed out on the rocks and bumps.

The road curved gently through the woods, and when Jeff didn't see the station after two hundred yards, he started to wonder if he'd taken the wrong laneway in. But then, there it was!

The trees opened up and the railroad station was there before him.

'Okay, pal,' Jeff said to the dog. 'We're here.'

He jumped out of the truck, came around to the other side, opened the door and once again carefully scooped the dog into his arms. He was a dead weight, totally limp, but he probably wasn't much more than twenty or thirty pounds, so he wasn't hard to carry.

While he felt even more comforted in the boy's arms, Chipper now wondered whether he had made a mistake. He didn't want those people from The Institute finding him here and putting the boy in danger. But when the truck had bumped him, he'd sensed that anything The Institute might be using to track him had been disabled.

He hoped so.

Jeff got the station door open. As he stepped inside, a tiny, grey mouse scurried along one of the dirty baseboards and out of sight. He slowly carried the dog up the stairs to the second floor, careful not to press hard on the steps Emily had said were weak, and set him in the oversized beanbag chair that Emily had told him was her special place. Jeff reshaped the chair slightly so the dog wasn't curled up in a hole.

'You just take it easy,' he said. 'I'm going to get you something to eat and drink and try to find out who you belong to.'

Chipper studied the boy with his brown eyes, which Jeff noticed had an odd quality about them. Chipper knew his eyes would appear strange to anyone who looked at them closely, that they did not look entirely *natural*. He blinked his eyes – something he didn't actually need to do – to break the boy's attention on them.

Chipper felt, for the first time since his escape, not just happiness. He felt a sense of hope. Without even having to think about it, he managed to convey that to Jeff.

'Hey!' said Jeff. 'You're wagging your tail!'

Just a little, Chipper thought. *You should see how much I can wag it when I'm feeling better.*

'Yes!' Jeff said. 'This is great!'

He dropped to his knees, cradled the dog's head in his arms, felt the soft fur of his ears on his palms, and put his face right up to the dog's. 'I am going to do everything I can to help you. But I have to go now. I'm going to be back real soon.'

Do you have to go? Chipper thought. *Can't you stay here with me? After all I've gone to, to find you?*

Jeff raced down the stairs and out of the station. He decided to leave his aunt's truck by the station, and hightailed it through the woods to Emily's house at Shady Acres. He put his nose to the screen door, peering inside, as he rapped on the frame. When no one answered, he ran towards the lake, where he found Emily sitting on the end of a dock, dangling her feet in the water.

'Hey!' he shouted. But she didn't turn around. As he got closer, he could see that she was listening to music, but when he ran out onto the dock, she pulled the buds from her ears, wound them up and tucked them into her pocket.

'You have to come with me!' he said.

'What? Where?'

'To the station.' He took a couple of deep breaths. 'You have to come.'

'What is going on with you?'

'We need water, and some food. Like, do you have any hot dog wieners? Or some raw meat? Like some hamburger? And water! Yes, we need water!'

'Are we having a picnic? Because if we are, I am definitely not into raw meat.'

'No, not a picnic. Come on, come on. You're wasting time!'

'Stop talking and tell me what's happening!'

Jeff blinked. 'Which do you want? For me to stop talking, or to tell you what's happening?'

Emily gave him a look of total exasperation. 'Just tell me.'

'I found a dog. He ran in front of the truck. I don't think I hit him hard, but he's hurt and I took him to the station.'

'Whoa,' Emily said. 'Why didn't you just take him to your place?'

'My aunt *hates* dogs.'

She thought a moment. 'We could tell my dad.'

Jeff shook his head. 'Do you think, if we can't find the owner, he'd want to adopt a dog?'

Emily slowly shook her head. 'He's got like a huge dog allergy.'

'Then he's either going to tell my aunt, or make us take it to the dog pound.'

'What's all this *us* stuff?'

'Are you going to help me or not?'

She took a moment to think it over, then said, 'Fine. Let me see what I can get from the fridge. Wait here.'

Emily got her feet out of the water, slipped her shoes back on, and ran back up the hill to her house. Jeff stood on the dock and gazed out over Pickerel Lake.

Aunt Flo was going to wonder why it was taking him so long to do a simple run to the dump. There were times Jeff wished he could put her in the truck and leave *her* there.

If Jeff couldn't find out who owned that dog, she'd never let him keep it. She'd made him give up one dog and he wasn't going to let her do it again.

Emily came running back down the hill with a plastic bag full of stuff. 'Okay,' she said. 'Let's go. I didn't have to tell Dad anything. He's been clearing some brush and is going to run it to the dump. I just hope he doesn't notice that he's down one T-bone steak when he gets back. If he finds out I took it he'll kill me.'

They headed into the woods, and as the station and his aunt's pickup truck came into view, Emily said, 'What's that smell?'

'Oh,' Jeff said. 'I was on my way to the dump when I found the dog. The truck's full of garbage.'

She made a face. 'Barf City.'

As they entered the old station, Jeff asked Emily what was in her bag, beside a steak.

'Bottled water, some crackers, peanut butter, some cheese and some Rice Krispie squares.'

'Do dogs eat Rice Krispie squares?' he asked.

'They're for us, bozo,' she said.

Heading up the stairs, he said, 'I hope you won't mind, but I put him in your chair. I couldn't put him on the flat floor. I wanted him to be comfortable.'

'Fine.'

They hit the top of the stairs and turned to look into the room.

There was Emily's beanbag chair.

But the dog was gone.

Aunt Flo strode up to Cabin Eight and rapped on the door hard.

'Mr Green?' she called. 'Mr Green, are you in there?'

She put her face right up to the screen door and peered inside. Harry Green slowly lumbered into view and pushed the door open.

'What is it, Flo? I was just having a little nap.'

'Have you seen that damn fool nephew of mine?' she asked.

'Uh, like I said, I was having a nap before I go back out to catch absolutely nothing. Is there a problem?'

'He went off to the dump a long time ago and he's not back yet.'

'Haven't seen him. I'm sure he's fine.'

'Oh, I'm sure he is. But I've got a long list of things that need doing. I took that boy in. I'm giving him a place to stay and feeding him and keeping clothes on his back. Doesn't seem to be asking too much to have him do a few things in return.'

'He's been through a lot,' Harry said. 'Losing his mother and father. And so tragically, too.'

She softened some. 'I suppose.' She decided to change the subject. 'You enjoying your first summer here?'

'Oh, yes, very much.'

'How'd you hear about my place?' Flo asked.

Harry Green furrowed his brow. 'Someone must have mentioned it at work one time and it just stuck in my head.'

'What sort of work did you do?'

'Oh, a bit of this and that,' Harry said. 'Nothing very interesting. What did you say Jeff's parents did? Worked for some drug company?'

'Something like that,' Flo said. 'Heck of a thing, what happened to them. Jet blowing up in mid-air over the water. It was some kind of engine failure. Or something with the electronics. That's why I don't fly.'

'Let me ask you this, Flo,' Harry said. 'Have there ever been any people coming around here, asking about Jeff, checking up on him?'

'What do you mean?'

Harry shrugged. 'Just what I said. People dropping by, maybe people his parents used to work with, asking how he is, whether there is anything they can do to help?'

Flo shook her head. 'Nope, nothing like that. Were you thinking there would be?'

135

'I don't know,' Harry said. 'Just asking.'

'I'd still like to know where he's gone off to. You sure you've got no idea? I see Jeff talking to you now and then.'

Harry gave her a sly smile. 'If I were a betting man, I'd say a girl might be involved.'

'Oh for heaven's sake,' Flo said. 'That's all we need.'

20

'He was right here!' Jeff told Emily, pointing at her beanbag chair. 'I left him right here in this chair!'

'Uh, huh,' she said dubiously, holding the bag of food she'd taken from her house.

There wasn't any place for the dog to have hidden upstairs here, which meant he had to have gone downstairs. But the door was closed when they got here. Jeff went back down to the main floor, ran through what was once the waiting room for passengers, poked his head into the former office, looked behind the counter where, decades ago, people once stood selling tickets.

He even looked in the old bathroom where stained and rusted toilets sat disused in stalls.

Jeff didn't see the dog anywhere.

But he did discover one busted window over behind the ticket counter. The glass had been shattered at some point, leaving teeth-like shards around the edges. There was an old, broken chair and desk in front of it, so it wouldn't have been hard for the dog to use them as steps to get up to the window.

There was a wisp of black fur, and blood, on one of the glass shards.

'Oh, no,' Jeff said, pointing.

'Crap,' said Emily.

Once outside, Jeff called out: 'Dog! Hey, dog! Come on, boy! We've got food for you!'

'Shh!' Emily said. 'I hear something.'

Jeff went quiet and held his breath. There were the usual forest sounds. A rustling of leaves, a breeze blowing through the trees.

And something else. A kind of grunting.

'I think it's coming from the truck,' Emily said.

Jeff turned in the direction of the pickup. 'Something's in the back,' he said. 'With the garbage.'

They approached the truck cautiously. Jeff knew there were plenty of other creatures that could be in the truck. Raccoons, foxes, a skunk – even a bear was a possibility. Any one of those animals might be interested in feasting on that trash.

The good news was, Jeff didn't see any big, black, furry bear's head sticking up over the sides of the cargo bed.

The bad news was, he saw blood on the side of the top edge of the tailgate.

Emily and Jeff moved around to the back of the truck, heard more rustling and grunting noises. 'Stand back,' Jeff said, approaching the tailgate. He slipped his fingers under the handle and got ready to pull as Emily took three steps back.

Jeff dropped the tailgate in one swift motion.

The dog, his butt to them, whirled around suddenly. He'd managed to pull one can over and had had his snout deep into a bag of trash. If a dog could look terrified, well, that was how he looked when he saw them. Eyes wide, jaw open. There was fresh blood matted into the fur of his belly. 'It's okay!' Jeff said. 'It's me!' He pointed to Emily. 'That's Emily! She brought food!'

Chipper looked at Emily and tried to assess whether she was a friend or a foe. Dogs, even dogs without a few million dollars' worth of software built into them, often had an instant sense of people, and Chipper was no different.

He thought Emily was probably okay, especially when she raised the bag in her hand and smiled.

'So you don't have to eat this yucky stuff, okay?'

Emily dug into the bag and brought out something wrapped in freezer paper. 'Wait'll you see this,' she said. 'It was going to be my dad's Sunday night dinner.' She ripped through tape and unfolded the paper to reveal the steak. 'Bet you'll like this.'

Chipper's mouth instantly watered. That steak looked even better than those wieners he'd stolen from the barbecue. Emily tore off a chunk of it and extended it in her hand. Chipper gave it a sniff, then gently took it from her palm, being careful not to bite her.

Two quick bites, a gulp, and it was gone.

Not bad, Chipper thought. Better than that cheap stuff they gave him at The Institute.

Jeff put a hand close to the bloody fur without actually touching it. 'You did that going through the window – didn't you, you dumb dog, you?'

Chipper eyed him with tired, sorrowful eyes. He'd found enough strength to get out of that beanbag chair, jump through a window, and hop into the back of this truck for something to eat, but now he felt very weary. He was starting to waver.

'I think maybe you got up too soon,' Jeff said. 'Whaddya say we take you back up to the comfy chair and give you a little more to eat and drink and we take a look at that cut?'

Jeff put one arm around his front legs, just under his neck, and the other around his back, tucking his tail in as he did it. Chipper made no objections. Emily followed them back into the train station and up the stairs, where Jeff gently placed him back in the chair, his head resting over the edge.

Emily got out everything else she had in the bag. She'd brought two bottles of water, cracking one open immediately. 'I'm an idiot. I should have brought a bowl.' But when she tipped the top of the bottle up to Chipper's mouth, he managed to drink it. She gave him more of the steak and a piece of cheese while Jeff looked at the cut on his stomach.

'We need to get some bandages and stuff,' he said.

Chipper wanted to tell them it wasn't that bad. He wanted to tell them a lot of things. Maybe, before too long, they'd find an opportunity.

'I'll start making a list of the things we need,' Emily said. 'Bandages, a bowl, a brush to comb out his fur, which is all natty and totally a mess.' She got out her phone, opened some app she could make notes on, and tapped away with her thumb.

'Write down a board and some nails,' Jeff said. 'We don't want him jumping out the window again, or anything bad getting in.'

Won't do that, Chipper thought. *Want to stay with you.*

Emily said, 'I can only get so much in one trip. We can fix the window another time.'

The dog had swallowed his steak and cheese, so Emily gave him some more.

His tail softly thumped.

'You said you checked his collar for a tag?' she asked Jeff.

'Didn't see anything.'

'Let me have a closer look. Hey, fella, just want to check your collar there.'

Emily worked her fingers under the black fur, found the collar and ran her fingers around it.

Emily looked puzzled. 'This is strange,' she said.

'What?'

'Well, you're right, there's no tag, but the collar is super tight. I can't get my finger under it anyplace.'

'He must be choking,' Jeff said.

'Yeah, but, his neck doesn't feel all squished or anything. It's like – this is totally strange – but it's like the collar is stuck right to his body.'

'Let me try.'

Jeff got his fingers on the collar and confirmed what Emily was saying. 'You're right. It's sort of like the collar is part of him. Maybe it's like, when you wear a ring for years, your finger kind of grows around it. My mom's finger was like that.'

'Why would anyone put a collar on a dog that tight? That just seems like such a mean thing to—'

'Whoa,' Jeff said. 'Hang on.'

'What?'

'There's something . . . there's something weird on this collar. In fact, this whole collar is kind of weird.'

'How?'

'It feels like . . . metal.'

Emily brushed her hands up against Jeff's as she gave the collar another feel. 'I see what you mean.'

Jeff put her hand in his – and felt a bit of a shiver when he did – and moved it to the part of the collar on the right side of the dog's neck. 'Feel that.'

Emily did. 'That feels like a . . .'

'Like a what?'

'I'm not going to say. You'd think I was insane. I have to *see* it.'

She gently moved Chipper over onto his other side, spread the fur apart the way you might part someone's hair, looking for a bump on the head. She exposed the collar, which was dark silver and had a soft sheen to it, then zeroed in on what she'd been looking for.

'I don't believe it.'

'What? I can't see it.'

'It's an opening,' Emily said. 'It's a port.'

'A port? What do you mean, a port?'

'Like you'd plug a computer into, or an iPhone, or a USB stick.'

Jeff looked closer at what Emily'd found. 'That *is* insane,' Jeff said. 'It *is* a port. But where does it go?'

Emily touched Jeff's shoulder so he'd turn and look at her. 'It goes right into the dog,' she said.

'But why . . . why would anyone do something like that? Why would a dog have a slot to plug a computer into?'

'I guess I'll go get my computer,' Emily said, 'and we'll find out.'

21

Jeff stayed with the dog while Emily ran back to her place for a laptop computer and a cable. The whole idea of what they were about to try seemed crazy. They were actually going to plug a computer into a dog?

But then Jeff thought, no, they weren't plugging a computer into a dog. They were just plugging a computer into a dog's *collar*. Maybe that wasn't quite so weird. They made computers so small these days, you could probably fit all kinds of stuff into that band that ran around the dog's neck.

After all, couldn't you implant a little GPS chip in your pet these days, so that if it went missing, you could find it? Yeah, that made sense. Of course, you couldn't really connect to that chip, but maybe this was some variation on that. By putting the chip in the collar, you didn't have to actually break the dog's skin, which, when you think about it, is not a very nice thing to do to a dog or a cat or even a gerbil.

That's probably all this was, Jeff figured. Just a

fancy locater for somebody's pet. And once Emily was back here with her computer, and plugged it into that collar, they'd know who this dog belonged to and could organise a reunion.

The thought of which made Jeff a little sad.

He hadn't spent a lot of time with this dog, but he liked him. He liked him a *lot*. But the boy had to face reality. Even if this dog turned out to belong to nobody, there was no way he was going to be able to keep him. Not with Aunt Flo hating pets.

And speaking of Aunt Flo . . .

She must be having six fits that he still hadn't returned. He hadn't even *gotten* to the dump yet. He was wondering what he'd tell her. The dump was closed? He'd had to go to one in a different county? Flat tyre?

Alien abduction?

The dog turned his head slightly and looked up at Jeff from his spot on the beanbag chair. 'How ya doin', buddy?' Jeff asked.

The dog's tail thumped with slightly more energy this time.

'I guess I never actually introduced myself,' the boy said. 'My name is Jeff.'

Another thump of the dog's tail.

'Jeff Conroy. I'm twelve years old, and I live with my aunt, whose name is Flo. She's my dad's sister, or was my dad's sister, I guess, since my dad is dead. I guess she's still my dad's sister, even if he is dead. I don't

145

know. Anyway, I live with her because both my mom and my dad are dead. It happened last year. Their names were Edwin and Patsy. Edwin is kind of a strange name. You don't hear it that much. Patsy is sort of normal, although it sounds kind of old-fashioned. I think it's kind of a nickname for Patricia, which was my mom's proper name on her birth certificate. Well, I guess it would have been on her *death* certificate, too. And the girl who's been helping me and who got you all the food is Emily Winslow. She's kind of okay, considering when I first met her I thought she was kind of a snot.'

Jeff had no idea just how closely the dog was listening to his every word, understanding him, even feeling sad for him.

'So I help my aunt run her business, and I really, truly hate my life,' Jeff said. 'I miss my parents, and I also miss a dog I had once, named Pepper. My aunt made me get rid of him. The only thing that's made me kind of happy in a long time is finding you.'

The dog twisted his snout towards Jeff and raised his head.

'What?' Jeff said, leaning closer, then gave a little start of surprise when the dog licked him, touching his chin and going right up over his lips, catching the tip of his nose.

'Hey,' Jeff said, and hugged the dog's head.

Jeff wasn't sure how long they would have stayed like that, but then they heard a noise downstairs. They both jumped and turned their heads to the top of the stairs.

'It's me!' Emily cried, running up the steps. She had a computer bag slung over her shoulder. She slid it off and unzipped it in one fluid motion, brought out the computer and put it in her lap after sitting cross-legged on the floor in front of her beanbag chair.

The dog watched her closely.

She drew a cord out of the case, plugged one end into the side of the laptop, and handed the other end to Jeff.

'Plug in the dog,' Emily said.

'Aye, aye, captain,' Jeff said. He parted the dog's fur once again, found the port, and connected the cord to it. 'It fits.'

'Of course it fits,' Emily said. 'You think I don't know my stuff?'

'I'm clearly not as into computers as you are.'

She didn't look at Jeff. She was staring at her screen. 'Okay,' Emily said, more to herself than to Jeff. 'Tap here . . . click here . . . and . . . nuts.'

'What?'

Jeff scurried around on his knees and looked over Emily's shoulders. He pointed and said, 'What is that?'

'Okay, so the computer has detected whatever program is in that collar, but it's asking for a password before I can get in.'

'Whoa. So there really *is* something in there.'

147

'Well, I guess,' Emily said. 'Maybe he's like a doggie bank machine. Before he gives us any money we have to know the PIN.'

Jeff ignored that. 'You'd think if that connection is there so that we can find out whose dog this is, his owner wouldn't want to slow you down with a password. They'd *want* you to get in, wouldn't they?'

'Maybe . . . They seem to be asking for five digits here.'

'So, like, we pick a number between zero, zero, zero, zero, zero, and nine, nine, nine, nine, nine?'

She half turned her head, not far enough to see Jeff, just far enough to make a face that he could see. 'Helpful,' she said.

The dog began to bark.

'*Arf! Arf arf arf!*'

'What is it, sport?' Jeff asked. 'You want something else to eat?' He reached for the bag Emily had brought earlier, dug out a cracker, and put it close to the dog's mouth.

He turned his snout away.

'Maybe with some cheese?' Jeff said, reaching back into the bag.

'*Arf!*'

Then a pause.

'*Arf arf arf!*'

Then another pause.

'*Arf arf!*'

Yet another pause.

'*Arf arf arf arf arf arf arf!*'

'What's with you?' Jeff asked.

Finally: '*Arf!*'

'Quiet!' Emily said, raising her head and shouting at the mutt. 'I'm thinking here! Trying to figure out if there's some way around this password.'

Jeff waved some cheese in front of the dog's nose but he rejected it just as he had the cracker.

'*Arf!*'

'*Arf arf arf!*'

'*Arf arf!*'

'*Arf arf arf arf arf arf arf!*'

'*Arf!*'

'He's driving me crazy,' Emily said. 'He doesn't make a sound for ages and now he's giving me a headache. Do you want us to find your owner or not?'

Jeff decided to eat the piece of cheese himself. 'What kind of cheese is this?' he asked Emily.

'Huh? It's havarti.'

'It's good.'

'*Arf!*'

'*Arf arf arf!*'

'*Arf arf!*'

'*Arf arf arf arf arf arf arf!*'

'*Arf!*'

The dog was looking right at Jeff, who realised that he seemed pretty agitated. A far cry from a few moments earlier, when the dog was licking Jeff's face.

Emily stared in puzzlement at her screen as the dog began to bark again.

'*Arf!*'

'*Arf arf arf!*'

'*Arf arf!*'

'*Arf arf arf arf arf arf arf!*'

'*Arf!*'

'Hang on,' Jeff said very slowly to Emily.

'What?'

'Enter one, three, two . . . uh, seven, and then . . . one.'

Chipper started to wag his tail while Emily scowled at Jeff. 'You just making this up?'

'Just . . . try it and see what happens.'

Emily typed in the series of numbers he'd given her, held her finger over the return/enter key, then came down on it hard.

She stared, bug-eyed, at the screen.

'It worked,' she whispered. 'How did you know? How could you possibly know?'

'The dog told me,' Jeff said.

'No, really, how did you know?'

'I'm serious,' Jeff said. 'His barks. He was barking out a series of numbers.'

Emily's mouth hung open. 'That's totally nuts,' she said. 'And yet . . . I'm in.'

'In where, exactly?'

Jeff was back to looking at the screen with her. There was a lot of white space, kind of like the space on a smart phone before you start texting. At the top was a row of buttons, all with different tiny icons.

'I still don't believe you,' Emily said. 'There's no way the dog—'

'Look,' Jeff said.

Something was happening on the screen. Letters were starting to appear. Letters that turned into words, and then an entire sentence. Four, in fact.

Jeff is not lying, Emily. I gave him the password. I was starting to think you would never figure it out. Way to go!

They both looked from the screen to the dog. He was staring right at them.

Then, more words on the screen.

Hi! My name is Chipper.

The dog fixed his eyes on the boy.

I am so glad I finally found you. I need your help!

22

Back at The Institute, Wilkins was very concerned about doing his job properly. There'd been rumours going around all day about what had happened to Simmons. He had displeased Madam Director, and no one had seen him since.

Of course, Simmons *had* screwed up big time. He'd let H-1094, the animal known around the lab as Chipper, get away. Big, big mistake. It was bad enough that the animal had failed to live up to its potential. But at least a defective hybrid could be treated like a wrecked car. It could be harvested for its parts. And there were a great many of them in H-1094. The dog's eyes alone were worth more than four million dollars. They could be used again in another animal. Same for a lot of the other implanted hardware. The GPS, the recording system, the software that allowed such a primitive creature to *think*.

To communicate.

That had to be the single most astonishing

achievement at The Institute. Finding a way to let the animal communicate with you. Giving it the power – not of speech, exactly – but of turning its thoughts into words so it could provide information. You could put a dog out into the field and have it record things for you, allow it to be your eyes and ears, but sometimes you needed your operative (and that's really what Chipper and the others were: *operatives*) to just tell you what was happening. Not everything could be interpreted from the data that came into the control room. You needed some *judgement*, and that had been built into the programming. You didn't want the dogs to tell you *everything* that was going on around them, just the things that *mattered*.

What they'd done, in effect, was given the dog a second brain. An artificial intelligence that had melded with the dog's own cognitive abilities and instincts.

It just hadn't worked the way it should with Chipper. Those canine instincts too often came to the fore.

Still, they'd accomplished a lot within this building. Even if Chipper hadn't worked out, many of the other animals looked promising, and once they'd perfected the process with the dogs, then they could move on to—

No, best not to even think about that. Many of the people working here weren't even supposed to *know* about the next step. Some employees who'd been privy to the long-term goals of The Institute and had raised ethical and moral concerns were no longer getting a pay cheque.

In fact, Wilkins had reason to believe those employees no longer *existed*.

You couldn't have someone going to the *New York Times* or CNN with tales of what was going on here. Wilkins had never even told his own wife the truth about the kind of work he did. Sharon believed he worked in a medical facility, reading patient X-rays. There was no way he could ever tell her what he was up to. The biggest challenge every day was preparing conversational stories to tell her over dinner. He had created a small, fictional universe about his workplace, invented names for colleagues, given them back stories filled with gossip. It had seemed like a good idea at the time, but now Sharon wanted to meet these people. Have them over for dinner, maybe get together for drinks.

That was not happening.

And even if it ever did, Sharon was *never* going to meet Simmons.

Simmons had seriously underestimated Chipper. The dog even used his security card to get away! When Chipper had escaped, very little of his software was operational. Rebooting it from the control room had been difficult, particularly when the animal had been in some kind of metal container, which, he later learned, was the luggage hold on that bus.

But once the dog had fled the bus station, Wilkins had gone back to work on the GPS issue, as well as

154

trying to activate the visuals. The animal's eyes not only allowed it to see where it was going, it let The Institute see what it was looking at. Planted into Chipper's retina was a camera lens no larger than the head of a pin. All Wilkins had to do was make a few computer clicks to bring the camera into operation to see what the dog saw.

Wilkins had been having some trouble getting that going, too.

And just when he thought he had the GPS fully operational – he had managed to locate the dog in the general area of some garbage dump outside Canfield – it went out. Just like that! In the midst of all these thoughts, Wilkins suddenly sensed a presence behind him.

He turned away from his computer screen and there, towering over him on her four-inch heels, was Madam Director, arms folded across her chest, eyeing him sternly through her black-rimmed glasses.

'Give me some good news, Wilkins,' she said.

'Yes, well, I was just in touch with Daggert on the scene to tell him of an approximate location of H-1094. After that I lost the GPS but I'm working on that and a visual feed.'

'Define *working on*.'

'Well, uh, you know, working my darnedest to get it up and running as fast as I can.'

'How long?' she asked.

'I, uh, am not sure. Any second now, I hope.'

'Hope,' Madam Director said. 'We don't run on hope here, Wilkins. We run on results.'

'Of course, of course. Let me, uh, let me just see what I can do here.'

Wilkins began frantically tapping and clicking. 'What I was thinking is, if we can get the visuals up and running and we can view the surroundings, that will help us with location while we work on the GPS.'

Droplets of sweat sprouted on Wilkins's brow. He could sense others at nearby stations working hard not to look at him. They were completely focused on their own duties, praying the Director would not choose to look over their shoulders next.

'Hang on, hang on,' he said. 'I think we may have the lens in the right eye coming on here.'

Having both cameras – one for each eye, of course – provided better images and depth of field, but to have even one working would be a bonus.

'Here we go!' he said.

There was static at first, then jagged horizontal bars, then an image. It moved for half a second, then froze.

'This is supposed to be live video, yes?' Madam Director asked.

'That's right.'

'What you have there is not video, Wilkins. It's an image. A picture. It's frozen.'

'Yes, yes, I can see that, but—'

'What is it, anyway?'

At first, Wilkins wondered if the dog might be looking in a mirror, because what was looking back at them was an eye.

A big eye.

But it wasn't a mirror. If it were a mirror, there'd be black and white fur surrounding that eye. Maybe a snout, and a black nose.

This eye was framed by an eyebrow across the top, a hint of an ear to the right, and a tiny bit of nose to the left.

This was a human being. Face to face with Chipper.

'Where is this?' Madam Director demanded.

'I can't tell,' Wilkins said. 'I can't see anything beyond this bit of face. It could be indoors, outdoors. It could be anywhere.'

Madam Director leaned over Wilkins, got her own face to within a foot of the screen.

'That,' she said slowly, 'is a boy.'

23

'This is not happening,' Emily said. 'This dog—'

'His name is Chipper,' Jeff said, pointing to the screen of her laptop. 'He just told you right there.'

'This *Chipper* is not talking to us,' she said. 'This is some kind of a joke. Someone is playing a trick on us.'

Emily tipped her head back and said, in a loud voice, 'Whoever you are, very funny!'

Words came up on her screen.

Not a joke! This is for real!

'Who's your owner?' Jeff asked Chipper. 'Who's your, you know, master?'

You!

'No, no, you don't understand. Who looks after you? Where's your home?'

Can this be my home? I like it here. Lots of things to smell.

'Um, well, this is just an old abandoned train station. You must have come from a better place than this?'

'Stop,' Emily said. 'This is nuts. Dogs don't talk.'

'He's not *talking*,' Jeff said. 'He's *communicating* with us. A talking dog, well, that *would* be nuts.'

'This is nuts, too!' Emily said.

'Then how do you explain it? You found that port, you wanted to check it out, you got your laptop. And now we're having a conversation with Chipper.'

'With a *dog*.'

A different kind of dog!

'What do you mean?' Jeff asked. 'You look like a dog. Are you a computer?'

Part computer, part dog!

'What did you mean when you said you wanted us to help you?'

They are chasing me.

'Who's chasing you?'

White Coats! They want to end me.

'You mean . . . kill you?' Jeff said. Emily, who'd been rolling her eyes a few moments ago, was now giving Chipper her full attention.

Yes!

'Why would these guys in white coats want to kill you?'

I got away. I hid on a bus. I found you!

'You mean, more like I found you,' Jeff said. 'I nearly killed you with the truck! You really, really scared me.'

I am okay. There are things you have to do. Fast!

'Like what?' Jeff said.

159

Turn things off.

'What things? What things have to be turned off?'

Emily said, 'He must be talking about these settings. There's all these icons and stuff across the top of the screen.'

'So, you don't think it's a joke any more?'

'I don't know what to think. But I can tell you I've got a pretty bad feeling about all this. I think I should tell my dad.'

'Your dad?'

'He used to be a cop.'

No!

'What do you mean, no?' Jeff said to the dog.

No police. They will know!

'He's not a cop *now*,' Emily said. She shook her head. 'I can't believe I'm arguing with a dog.'

Jeff said to her, 'You're way smarter than I am with computers. Study that thing. Turn off anything that looks like it connects to these white coat dudes he's talking about.'

Yes! Do that!

Emily studied the screen, did some clicking. 'Okay, I think I know what to do here.'

To Chipper, Jeff said, 'Okay, let me try to figure this out. Who are the white coat guys?'

They run The Institute.

'The Institute? What's The Institute? Is that, like, a community college or something?'

160

Secret place.

'Like a government agency or something?'

Chipper nodded his head several times.

'This is where they turned you into some kind of computer dog? And you escaped because they were going to kill you? And now they're looking for you?'

Very good! That is it!

'Do they know where you are?'

They know I am in this area.

'Holy crap,' Jeff said.

Emily said, 'Okay, I found the GPS thingamabob, and I've turned it off. It didn't look like it was working, but now it's not going to come back on. And there's this thing called "video link" that's kind of flashing on and off like it's trying to work.'

Jeff leaned in close to Chipper, nose to nose. 'It's going to be okay,' he said, looking into his eyes. 'We're going to protect you.'

Chipper wasn't so sure, but he did not want to tell them that. At that moment, he felt his left eye do something. He knew, immediately, what was happening. He wanted to close his eye, to close off the view, but his internal workings wouldn't allow it. But he was pretty sure Emily could do it if she just clicked the right things.

To Jeff, the eye seemed to twinkle. There was a spark, and then it was gone. He stepped back and looked again at the screen to see what Emily was up to.

'Okay,' Emily said, 'I just killed the video link. Now there's something here labelled "base connect". Let me just see . . .'

Turn off!

'Chipper says turn that off,' Jeff said.

'I can see the screen, Jeff.'

'Oh, yeah, sorry.'

'I think all the things that connect him to anybody else have been disengaged,' Emily said.

Jeff breathed a sigh of relief. 'I want to try to do something here,' Emily said. 'I can't haul a laptop everywhere, but we want to know what he's saying. I think I can configure this so what he says will show up on my phone, and I won't need a wire.'

Great idea!

'And I've got a phone back at the camp, too,' Jeff said. 'Can we set up mine, too?'

Emily nodded. 'I think so.'

'What I figure I should do,' Jeff said, 'is get that trash out of the truck, go back and come up with some kind of story for my aunt, then get my phone and get back here.'

'Sounds like a plan,' Emily said.

To Chipper, he said, 'I guess you heard all that. So I'll be back as soon as I can. But I have a question for you.'

Chipper looked at the boy expectantly.

'If these white coat guys who are looking for you – if they find you, and they find you with me and Emily, will we be in a lot of trouble?'

Chipper took a moment.

Not for long.

24

The big, black shiny SUV with deeply tinted windows came tearing up the gravel road that led into the dumpsite. It looked more like something that would be used for chauffeuring celebrities or government officials, not hauling bags of broken eggshells and dirty diapers and coffee grounds.

And, in fact, it was not hauling anything like that.

The SUV came to a stop, stirring up dust, and the driver's door opened. Daggert got out. Even with the sunglasses on, he made a visor of his hand to scan his surroundings.

He was looking for movement. Maybe a tail sticking up from behind a bag of trash.

Daggert wasn't about to get his own hands dirty. Or his beautifully polished black shoes, for that matter. So he looked into the SUV and shouted, 'Let's go!'

He had no problem sending Bailey and Crawford to traipse through the garbage looking for that dog. For now, this was still the best lead he had. Watkins or

Wilkins or whatever his name was had detected the dog in this area, and there'd been no new information since to lead Daggert anywhere else.

Bailey and Crawford got out of the vehicle and approached their boss. 'Yes?' said Crawford.

Daggert pointed directly at the heaps of smelly, disgusting garbage. 'Start looking.'

'In there?' Bailey asked.

Daggert gave her a look that did not invite further objection. His two assistants reluctantly waded into the garbage, tiptoeing, even though they were wearing shoes, as if that would somehow protect them.

Daggert stood by the SUV, driver door open, his cell phone resting on the top of the dash by the steering wheel. After five minutes he called out, 'Anything?'

Bailey's blond head appeared from behind a mountain of trash. She looked like she might throw up. 'A rat just tried to run up my pant leg,' she said.

Crawford, about forty feet away, stepping delicately around green bags that had been ripped open by seagulls, turned Daggert's way and shouted, 'I don't see any dog around here at all.'

'It's a big dump,' Daggert said. 'If he's here, and has seen us, he might be hiding. Start looking under some of that stuff.'

Bailey and Crawford stared at Daggert with a mix of disgust and disbelief. When they'd signed on to do the kind of nasty work that secret organisations demanded, they hadn't imagined they'd have to pick through stinky, gooey, disgusting garbage.

Daggert heard a vehicle approach and turned around.

A pickup truck was coming down the dirt road that led in from the gravel one. The truck was, not surprisingly, loaded down with trashcans. It drove up close to the pit, spun around, then backed up to it, all about twenty feet away from the black SUV. Daggert noticed some writing on the door.

Flo's Cabins.

The driver's door of the truck opened and a kid got out. Didn't look old enough to drive, Daggert thought.

The kid glanced over at Daggert briefly. Daggert had to admit to himself that he must have looked out of place. The boy hopped into the cargo bed and began upending the cans to let the trash spill out. When he spotted the well-dressed Bailey and Crawford wandering through the mounds of garbage, he did a double-take.

Daggert could remember back to when he was a kid himself. He and his friends would go to a local dump to shoot rats. Sometimes they'd even find the odd treasure. Stuff that was perfectly good that people didn't need any more and couldn't be bothered to try to sell. A bicycle one time, a boxful of old *Playboy* magazines another.

When Daggert thought the kid had been scoping out his associates for a few seconds too long, he called over to him and said, 'You got a problem?'

The boy's head turned. 'Excuse me?'

'I said, you got a problem?'

'No, sir,' he said. 'I just . . . I was just looking at those people. Are they with you?'

'Who wants to know?'

'I'm sorry. I'll mind my own business.' The boy went back to emptying trash barrels.

'Good idea,' Daggert said. 'You even old enough to drive?'

The kid banged the can on the edge of the tailgate in a bid to free some stubborn trash stuck to the bottom. He turned to Daggert and said, 'I guess. I mean, I drove here.'

'Oh, so you're a smartass. You got a driver's licence?'

The kid held the man's gaze. 'No, sir, I do not. I'm just trying to help my aunt run her business as best I can. If you want to arrest me, you won't be hurting me. You'll be hurting her.'

'I'm not going to arrest you. Do I look like a cop to you?'

'I don't know, sir.'

'Cops around here have big SUVs like this?' Daggert tucked his thumbs under his lapels. 'They dress like this?'

'I guess not.'

Bailey, unaware that her boss was in the middle of a conversation, shouted, 'Still no dog!'

'Same here!' said Crawford.

The boy blinked a couple of times. He swallowed, hard, and then asked, 'You lose your dog?'

'Yeah,' Daggert said slowly. 'You seen a dog on the loose around here?'

The boy shook his head from side to side quickly. 'No,' he said immediately.

'What, you've never seen a single dog running around here?' Daggert said. 'Would seem to me that a dog running around a place like this would be a pretty common occurrence.'

'I thought you meant, like, *lately*,' the boy said. 'I haven't seen any dog running around here *lately*.' He paused, then added, 'My aunt hates dogs. She won't let me have one.'

'She sounds like a nice lady,' Daggert said. He nodded at the words stencilled on the truck door. 'So, *Flo* is your aunt?'

'Yes, sir,' the boy said.

Daggert focused on the truck a moment longer. 'What's that?'

'What's what?' the boy replied.

'On the side of your truck. Looks like blood.'

The boy craned his neck over the side. 'Oh, yeah. Uh, I think some raccoons got into a fight in the truck the other night and one of them got hurt pretty bad.'

168

'Huh,' said Daggert.

The kid had one can left to go. He tossed an empty one back towards the cab window, grabbed the last can and hurriedly balanced it on the top of the tailgate and tipped. Even before all the trash had slid out, he put the can back into position, jumped out of the bed, and got back behind the wheel.

He didn't look at Daggert as he turned the ignition and drove away.

'Stupid kid,' Daggert said under his breath.

Bailey and Crawford trudged back to the SUV. Bailey said, 'Check with them again, see if they've got another fix on the dog. He's not in there. And even if he is, he's hid himself so well we'll never find him. At least not without help from the office. They've got to try and reconnect again.' She looked down at her feet. 'And I'd just like to say, I have ruined a three hundred dollar pair of shoes.'

'I'm gonna have to burn my suit,' Crawford said.

'Ah, that's sad,' Daggert said. 'Anyway, I'm inclined to agree with Bailey. We're not getting anywhere here. Let me make a call and—'

His hand was six inches from the phone when it started to buzz. Daggert snatched it off the dash and put it to his ear.

'I was just going to get in touch. We need you to—'

'Daggert, shut up.'

It was the voice of Madam Director. Daggert shut up.

169

'We may have something,' she said. 'I'm going to send you a picture. It's not a very good one, but I want you to look at it anyway.'

'Okay,' he said.

'I'm sending it to your car screen,' she said.

'One second,' Daggert said. He got behind the wheel and tapped a couple of buttons, bringing to life a tablet-size screen embedded in the dash. 'Ready.'

Madam Director could be heard talking to someone else. 'He's ready. Send it.'

Daggert kept his eyes on the screen. Suddenly, an image appeared.

'What the. . .?' said Daggert. 'It's an eye. Why are you sending me a picture of an eye?'

'Take a closer look,' Madam Director said.

'Okay, it's more than just an eye. There's an ear and part of a nose and an eyebrow. So it's not just an eye, it's part of a face. Where did this come from?'

'From the dog,' Madam Director said.

Daggert immediately understood. 'Okay,' he said. 'You've got a picture of somebody looking into the dog's face. How is that supposed to help me? I can't see any surroundings, anything that would tell me where this was taken.'

'I can tell you *when* it was taken. It was in the last hour.'

'I can't tell for sure,' Daggert said, 'but it doesn't look like an adult. That looks like a kid.'

'I agree,' Madam Director said. 'I think it looks like a boy.'

'Yeah, I think maybe—'

Daggert stopped himself in mid-sentence. He studied the image more closely.

'Daggert, are you there?'

He kept staring at the screen, even reached out and touched it with the tips of his fingers.

'Daggert!'

'Yeah, I'm here,' he said. 'I have to go.'

'Where are you going?'

'I'm going to see if Flo has any cabins available to rent.'

'What are you talking about? Who's Flo? Why do you want to rent a—'

But Daggert had already ended the call.

25

Emily was attempting to establish a link between Chipper and her phone so that the laptop would no longer be needed when having conversations. Chipper watched her intently, wagging his tail encouragingly. He wondered whether she was going to figure this out. She was very smart, no doubt about it, and if she were older, she had the brains to work at The Institute. *They could use more nice people like her*, he thought.

But if she was going to figure out how to talk with him using her phone, she needed to hurry up. Who knew how much time they had before the White Coats found him?

As Emily struggled with the laptop, words suddenly appeared on the screen.

Need help?

Emily looked at Chipper, and said, 'Seriously? You know how to synch a phone to your little computer brain?'

I know lots of things. Ask me anything.

Emily blinked. 'You gotta be kidding me. What are you? A flea-bitten Siri?'

I do not have fleas.

'Okay, sorry, didn't mean to offend you,' Emily said. 'All right, what's the capital of Rhode Island?'

Providence.

'Hmm,' Emily said. 'Maybe that was too easy. Let me think. Okay, I got it. Here's a great trivia question. What do you call this?' She touched her finger to the small indentation under her nose and above the middle of her upper lip.

Philtrum.

Emily stared at Chipper. 'You're freaking me out.'

Need help?

'Back to that, are we?'

Just asking.

'Fine, how do I do this?'

Go into Settings and click on 'Synching Auxiliary Device'.

'Okay, I'm there. Now what?'

Chipper led her through several steps. Finally, holding her phone and looking at the screen, she said, 'I think I've got it. Say something.'

I like to chase squirrels.

'Yes!' she said, grinning as the words appeared on the phone. 'It works!' But her grin quickly faded. 'So I get this working and you just want to talk about squirrels?'

No. I have other things on my mind. But it is true that I like to chase squirrels. Are there squirrels in these woods?

'Yes,' Emily said matter-of-factly. 'There are a lot of squirrels in these woods. There are hundreds of them. Thousands of them. They're all over the place.'

Okay.

'Do you think that's the most important thing we have to deal with right now?' Emily asked.

No.

Emily shook her head. 'This is like something out of a science fiction movie. Mixing up a dog and a computer. I mean, why would anyone even do that? What's the point? It must have cost millions to do what they did to you. Why? So you can open your own can of dog food?'

I would have been sent on missions.

'Missions? What do you mean, missions?'

To see things. Hear things. No one notices a dog.

'So, like, you're a spy? A *dog* spy?'

I get information. Does that make me a spy?

'I think so. I mean, how could a dog actually do what a spy does?'

I watch and record. I was going to be sent to foreign countries. Everything I saw and heard would be sent back.

'Who would you send it back to?' Emily said.

The White Coats. At The Institute.

'Yeah, right, okay. And they're part of the government?'

It took several seconds before Chipper came up with an answer, which turned out to be very short.

I do not know. I think I smell a raccoon on the roof!

'Focus, okay?' Emily was shaking her head. 'Why are you on the run?'

I was a failure.

'What do you mean, a failure?'

I like being a dog more than I like being a computer. I want to stop being a computer. I want to just be a dog.

Emily said, 'Really? I would think, if you're a half-dog, half-computer thingie, you have all these kinds of powers other dogs don't have. I think that would be cool. You're, like, a million times smarter than the other dogs. But here's the part I can't get my head around. You seem to have *feelings*. Like, when the stuff you say comes up on the screen, it sounds like you care about stuff.'

I do have feelings. All dogs have feelings.

'Well, sure, I guess,' Emily said. 'But yours seem more . . . I don't know how to explain it. They seem more kind of grown up.'

Chipper had nothing to say for a couple of minutes, so Emily continued with her technical efforts. There was something that was very much on his mind, even more than the prospect of getting out of the station and looking for animals. Finally, he asked a question.

Is Jeff a good friend?

Emily shrugged. 'I haven't really known him very long. But he seems okay. Why do you ask?'

Chipper did not answer. He was still thinking.

'What's the deal?' Emily asked. 'Are you rebooting or something? Why do you want to know if he's my friend?'

I have things to tell him.

'What?'

Things that may upset him.

'But you don't even know him.'

I know things about him. I knew I had to find him. I knew he would be kind to me.

'Okay, this is completely nuts. I mean, it's crazy enough, some robot dog that works for the government, but when you broke out you decided you had to find *Jeff*? Some kid who runs a fishing camp with his aunt? That's, like, pretty ridiculous.'

There are other things I need you to do.

'Like what? You mean, in your settings?'

Yes. I need more control over my defensive and logistical operations.

'Your *who*? I mean, your *what*?'

Chipper explained what he needed her to do. Emily searched through the various settings and made what changes she could.

'I hope that'll do it,' Emily said. 'What the heck is a "decibel distraction mode"?'

Something I might need. I have never used it before.

'Well, whatever it is, I think it's set to go. So, anyway, what's all this stuff you have to tell Jeff?'

He needs to know that

Chipper stopped mid-sentence.

There was the sound of an engine, and seconds later, a big bang from down below. Someone had burst through the door to the train station and was bounding up the stairs.

Screaming: 'They've found us! We have to get out of here!'

It was Jeff.

26

Only thirty minutes earlier, Aunt Flo had been standing in the middle of the driveway, out front of her house, fists on her hips, when Jeff arrived back into the camp from the dump. She looked like laser beams were about to come out of her eyes.

Jeff had a choice of hitting the brakes or running her down. He decided, with some reluctance, to slam on the brakes for the second time that day. The truck slid to a stop on the gravel. Aunt Flo's face was quickly at his open window, and she was angry.

'Where have you been? You've been gone nearly two hours! It doesn't take two hours to get to the dump and back! Where were you? What in blazes have you been up to?'

'I got held up,' Jeff said, hands gripped around the wheel.

'Held up? *Held up?* What's that supposed to mean? By bandits? Stagecoach robbers? There's all kinds of things that need doing around here and they're not getting done when you're goofing off.'

Jeff killed the ignition and slowly pushed open the door, giving his aunt time to back out of the way. He walked right past her and headed for the house.

'I'm talking to you!' she said.

'Aunt Flo, there's something I *really* have to deal with right now,' Jeff said. 'I'm sorry.'

He walked briskly and Aunt Flo struggled to keep up with him.

'What do you have to deal with that's more important than making sure my business runs efficiently?'

Jeff stopped and turned. 'I don't *care* about your business. I don't *care* about your stupid camp or your stupid cottages or your stupid boats and most of all I don't care about *you!*'

That stopped her dead in her tracks. Her mouth opened but nothing came out. Jeff was as stunned as she was. He couldn't believe he'd said those things, and instantly regretted them.

'I'm sorry,' he said. 'I didn't mean that. I mean, I did mean it, but I didn't mean to say it like that.'

Aunt Flo found her voice, and said, 'After all the wonderful things I have done for you.'

'Excuse me?'

'Taking you in, giving you a home after what happened to your mother and father. You think my life has been easy since you showed up?'

179

Her lip quivered. Jeff thought she looked like she might actually cry. He'd never believed, up until now, that she had the capacity to produce tears.

'It's not just about you, you know! Do you have any idea how much I loved your father? He was my baby brother, and I adored him! And maybe I didn't always get along with your mother, but I loved her, too. I know it was a hundred times worse for you, losing your parents, but I thought the world of them!'

Jeff didn't know what to say.

'You think I'm tough on you? Well, maybe I am,' she admitted. 'Do you think I do it just to be mean? You think I like yelling at you all the time?'

Jeff shrugged. 'Kinda.'

'Well, I don't!'

'You're yelling at me right now,' Jeff said.

She seemed to deflate, like a tyre losing some air. More quietly, she continued.

'Maybe I am. But you have to be strong. You're going out into the world without a mother or father to guide you, and if you're not tough, you'll get eaten alive.'

A tear emerged from her right eye and ran down her cheek. Jeff gazed upon it as if it were a flying cat. Not the kind of thing one saw every day.

'Okay, maybe I never wanted to be responsible for looking after you, but now I've got you, and you've got me, and we're stuck with each other.'

Jeff noticed, watching from a distance from behind the screen door of his cabin, his friend Harry Green.

'I never . . . I never understood,' Jeff said. 'But I still hate it here.'

That actually made Flo laugh. She did something Jeff couldn't remember her doing since he'd come to live with her. She held her arms out to him.

Really? She wanted to give him a hug?

Jeff stood frozen for a moment, then closed the distance between them and let her take him into her arms. Tentatively, he wrapped his arms around her in return. After three seconds, Aunt Flo disengaged herself.

'So, okay then,' she said, looking down at the grass as though embarrassed by her openness.

'Yeah, well,' Jeff said.

'Now, could you tell me why you were gone so long?' she asked, regaining her composure.

'No.'

'What?'

Jeff rested his hands on her shoulders. 'Aunt Flo, there's something I have to do right now that's very, very important, and I can't tell you, at least right now, what it's about. You just have to trust me. I will be back as soon as I can.'

'Where are you going?'

'I'm just running in to grab my phone, and then I

have to take off for a little while. I promise I won't be super long. If I run into a problem, I'll call you.'

'But—'

'No,' Jeff said firmly. 'There's something I have to do and I can't really explain what it is. You have to believe me.'

'But—'

Jeff gave her shoulders a squeeze. 'Please.'

Aunt Flo took a deep breath. 'Fine. But will you be here for dinner?'

'I don't know. Just save me something.'

She lowered her head slightly in an admission of defeat. Jeff gave her a quick kiss on the cheek, turned and ran into the house. He flew up the stairs in less than a second and dashed into his bedroom. He had left his cell phone charging on the bedside table. He detached it from the cord and shoved it down in the front pocket of his jeans.

He was just turning to his bedroom door when he heard a car – what sounded like a big car – barrelling down the driveway into the camp. He went to the window and stared in disbelief.

It was a big, black SUV.

The SUV came to a stop directly behind the Flo's Cabins pickup truck. Flo, who was still standing out front of the house, walked with a spring in her step towards it. She had several empty cabins – all cleaned and ready for guests! – so she put on her most welcoming smile.

With the engine still running, Daggert stepped out of the SUV. Seconds later, two other doors opened and Bailey and Crawford exited. They stood next to the vehicle, one on either side, while Daggert came up alongside the pickup, stopping to look at the door that featured the camp's name.

'How are you folks today?' Flo asked.

Daggert made a fist and pointed a thumb at the door. 'Are you Flo?'

'That I am,' she said, coming to within six feet of the man. 'You folks don't exactly look like you're dressed to go fishing, but if you're looking for a cabin, you're in luck! I just had a cancellation!'

She did not, after all, want to look desperate for

business. Let these folks think that they were lucky to find a vacancy.

Daggert eyed her from behind his shades. 'Where's the boy that was driving this truck?'

Flo blinked. 'Uh, is there some kind of problem?'

'I said, where's the boy that was driving this truck? You're his aunt, right?'

'Uh, yeah, I am. How did you know that?'

'Where is he?'

'Well, you can see that he's not in the truck, that much is for sure.'

Daggert took a step towards her. She tried to see his eyes behind the glasses, but couldn't make them out.

'Your nephew's in a heap of trouble,' Daggert said. 'You're going to be, too, if you don't tell me where he is.'

'If you could just tell me what this is about and who you people are, maybe I could help you with whatever your problem is.'

'Where's the dog?' Daggert asked.

'The what?'

'The dog. He's got the dog. Where is it?'

Flo shook her head and chuckled. 'Mister, if there's one thing I know for sure, it's that Jeff—'

'His name is Jeff, is it?'

'That's what I said. And I'm telling you, that if there's one thing I know, it's that Jeff does not have a dog. That's because I can't stand dogs.'

'That's what he told me,' Daggert said.

'So you've already talked?'

'We've met. Just because you don't think he's got a dog doesn't mean he doesn't.'

Flo crossed her arms and sized up Daggert, his two associates and their fancy car. 'You know, I get it now. You guys are the county's new dog-tag enforcement unit. I gotta say, you're the coolest-looking bunch of canine control officers I've ever laid eyes on.' Daggert glanced back at his aides, raised a hand into the air and snapped his fingers. They began to move.

'Hey, listen, I'm just kidding,' Flo said. 'I'm gonna tell you something and you better listen. My nephew's a good kid. Whatever you think he did, I'm sure he didn't mean it, or else he had a good reason to do whatever he did. If you guys can't even tell me who you are, then I don't see any reason why I have to answer your questions.'

'Search,' Daggert said to Bailey and Crawford.

Flo, without realising it, glanced at the house, then back to Daggert.

'Start there,' Daggert said, pointing.

'No, wait, stop!' Flo said. 'He went into town! Jeff borrowed my other car and drove into Canfield to get us some takeout for dinner! Honest! There's a great fish and chips place!'

Bailey and Crawford strode past her. Flo grabbed Bailey by the arm in a bid to slow her down but Bailey quickly shook her off.

'Stop,' Daggert told her as he reached into his jacket pocket.

'No! No! You stop! You've got no right! You can't go in that house! You – you need a warrant! I'm ordering you off my property! You get out of here! If you think you can search my house you better have a warrant in your hand!'

'Do I look like someone who worries about paperwork?' said Daggert, who was holding something that looked like a gun, but not quite. 'What the heck is that thing?' Flo asked.

'Allow me to demonstrate,' Daggert said, and jammed it into her side.

There was a sound like when a light bulb pops.

Flo went down.

She landed on the gravel driveway on her back, her right leg getting stuck behind her thigh, her left poking out at an odd angle.

She did not move.

Daggert knelt down beside her, touched two fingers to her neck, just under the jaw.

'Was worried I might have set it too high,' he said to himself. 'Sweet dreams, Flo.'

He left the woman there on the driveway and followed his two agents into the house.

28

When Jeff saw Aunt Flo drop to the ground, he had to put a hand over his mouth to stifle a scream.

A huge *NOOOOOOOO!* was about to burst from his throat as he stood at the second-floor window of his aunt's house, but he managed to hold it in as he jumped back from the window.

Jeff had had a funny feeling about that guy the moment he saw him at the dump. When he asked whether Jeff had seen a dog, he just *knew*. Chipper had been telling them the truth. He really was on the run, and there really were people looking for him.

Bad, *bad* people.

Jeff had overheard some of the conversation between his aunt and the man – enough to know they were looking for him and the dog.

He wondered how he'd given himself away. Was it written all over his face, when he'd been asked if he'd seen a dog around the dump? Was he that poor a liar? Or had they been tipped off some other way that the dog—

187

Whoa, wait a minute.

Chipper's eyes.

Just before Emily said she had killed the video link, there was this tiny spark in one of Chipper's eyes. Was it possible? Could the dog's eyes be cameras? Could they be a kind of window that those people, the ones who'd turned him into a weird hybrid thing, could see through?

If that was true, Jeff believed there was a good chance those people at The Institute had seen him.

Emily, too!

Given what had just happened to Aunt Flo, he knew these people would stop at nothing to get the dog back.

Call the police! a voice inside his head shouted.

Jeff got his thumb in position to hit 9-1-1 on the phone in his hand, then remembered Chipper's warning about telling Emily's ex-cop father.

No police. They will know!

These bad guys might be monitoring calls to the police! What had Chipper called them? The White Coats? These guys in the SUV were wearing dark suits, but it wasn't hard to imagine that they were all working together.

If calling the police wasn't safe, then what was Jeff going to—

They were heading for the house!

He bolted from his bedroom and was about to run down the stairs and sneak out the back door, but then he heard the front door opening. The stairs led right down to them.

'Crawford, Bailey, you check upstairs,' Jeff heard the lead guy say. 'I'll check down here.'

'Got it, Daggert.'

Daggert.

Jeff slipped across the hall and into Aunt Flo's bedroom. Her window opened onto a roofed porch. Once on the roof, he could grab one of the tall branches of an overhanging tree, and shimmy down to the ground.

He went to the window, grabbed it by the handles, and tried to lift it up.

It wouldn't budge.

He could hear two sets of footsteps on the stairs.

He pulled harder, but the window was stuck.

'You take those rooms, Crawford, I'll take these,' Jeff heard the woman – she had to be Bailey – say. He could tell they were at the top of the stairs.

That was when Jeff noticed the latch on the top of the window was still in the locked position. *Idiot!* He unlocked it, but there was no time now to open the window and slip out onto the roof without being seen.

Jeff dropped silently to the floor and rolled under his aunt's bed.

Someone came into the room.

Jeff turned his head towards the door and saw a dirty pair of women's shoes moving briskly down one side of the bed, then over to the window.

Please don't look under the bed. Please don't look under the bed.

The shoes didn't move for several seconds.

'Nothing over here!' Crawford shouted. It sounded like he was in Jeff's room across the hall.

'See if there's a way up into an attic or anything,' Bailey said.

Footsteps back in the hallway. Then, 'Yeah! There's a hatch in the hallway ceiling here!'

The woman moved hurriedly out of the room. That hatch was at the end of the hall, which meant Jeff had time to try the window again without being seen.

Crab-like, he moved out from under the bed, his front covered in matted balls of dust. For a second, he thought that it would only be a matter of time before Aunt Flo ordered him to vacuum under her bed.

Then he thought, *Not if she's dead.*

He went to the window and slid it open as far as it would go. He put his left leg out first onto the rooftop, ducked his head under and pulled the rest of his body outside. Stepping as noiselessly as possible – for all he knew, Daggert was standing right below him on the covered porch – he made his way to the corner of

190

the roof, where the branch of a tall oak was within easy reach.

Jeff grabbed it, swung off the roof, legs dangling, and edged his way the six to eight feet to the trunk.

Inside the house, Bailey called out, 'Was this window open before?'

Idiot! Jeff cursed himself again. But he had to keep moving.

He reached the trunk and scrambled down to a lower branch below the roofline. There was no outcropping to place his feet on, so he gently swung there.

The woman, louder this time – suggesting to Jeff she had her head sticking out the window – said, 'I could have sworn it was closed.' He was glad the leaves on the tree were so thick that they hid him from view.

Muffled, from inside the house, 'Are you gonna help me get into this attic or not?'

'Hang on,' she said.

Bailey could just as easily have been saying that to Jeff. He looked down, hoping to find a perch for his feet, but there was nothing there. So he dropped the rest of the way. It was only about eight feet, but real life isn't like the movies, where spies and superheroes jump off the top of buildings and do a little tuck and roll when they hit the ground and walk away like they'd just stepped off a kerb.

191

When his feet hit the ground he felt the shock go all the way up to his neck, as though his whole body had compressed a couple of inches. He scurried around the other side of the thick-trunked tree and held his breath, thinking that if anyone had seen him, he'd know in two seconds.

When no one came rushing out of the house, he figured they were all still in there. Bailey and Crawford were exploring the attic, and Daggert was probably skulking around the basement, expecting Jeff to be hiding behind the boiler. He moved from one tree to another, tiptoeing along like some cartoon character, then dashed for cover behind a row of shrubs, until he was back to his aunt's truck.

Only a few steps from Aunt Flo herself.

He was desperate to check on her, see if she was really dead, and get help for her if she wasn't – maybe the bad guys weren't monitoring calls for ambulances – but he'd be out in the open if he approached her. He couldn't risk it.

He crouched behind the passenger side of the truck where he could not be seen from the house, and peered in through the window. The keys were still in the ignition.

But hold on.

The black SUV nosed up behind it was making a lot of noise. Daggert had left it with the engine running.

Jeff quietly opened the passenger door on the pickup, leaned across the seat to the steering wheel, and took the key from the ignition. Then he moved back to the SUV, opened its passenger door, and got inside.

The windows were heavily tinted, so there was little risk that anyone would see him. There was a huge console between the two front seats that he had to climb over to get behind the wheel.

Jeff had only driven two motorised vehicles in his life: Aunt Flo's truck and her lawn tractor. No, wait. One time, his father had taken him to a go-kart track. But those experiences did not prepare him for this.

The seats were plush leather, there was a huge screen in the dashboard and there had to be like a million buttons all over the place. Now that Jeff had decided to use this as his getaway car, he wasn't sure how to make it go.

But how complicated could it be?

He got himself settled behind the wheel but found that his feet could not quite reach the pedals. That Daggert guy was a lot taller than Jeff. He reached under the front seat, looking for a lever to pull the seat forward, but there was nothing there. Then he ran his hand down the side of the seat and found a whole bunch more buttons. He pressed one and the back of the seat began to vibrate.

'What the—'

He tried another button and the seat began to lower. He did *not* want that! He could barely see over the dash as it was. He slid the button the other way and the seat went higher. He kept it going until he had a good view of the hood. Finally, he found the button that moved the seat forward and gave the gas pedal a nudge.

The car was so well sound-insulated that Jeff barely heard the engine respond. But respond it did. He was good to go.

The gear shift was in the console. Jeff pressed on the brake, moved the shift lever into reverse so he could back far enough away from Flo's pickup to turn around, and even though he felt he'd barely nudged the gas pedal, the SUV shot back like a rocket, pitching his head towards the steering wheel.

His foot found the brake and hit it hard. The SUV stopped abruptly, this time throwing Jeff's head into the headrest.

Jeff saw Daggert charge out the front door of the house and lock eyes on the SUV.

Jeff tromped on the gas and turned the wheel as sharply as it would go, clipping the corner of the pickup with a huge crashing noise. The car lurched hard to one side but Jeff kept pushing down on the accelerator. The back end fishtailed and it took him a second to get the SUV going in a straight line, but before he knew it, he was tearing back down the driveway and headed for the highway.

All Jeff had to do now was figure out what to do next.

29

Daggert's fists clenched at his side as he watched his SUV disappear beyond a ridge of trees. Bailey and Crawford burst out the door of the house several seconds later.

'Where's the car?' Bailey asked.

Daggert said nothing.

Crawford said, in a voice that sounded like he was trying to be helpful, 'I think, when you got out, you might have left the key in it.'

Daggert, turning slowly and giving the two of them a murderous look, said, 'Get the pickup.'

Bailey and Crawford glanced at each other, unsure which of them had been given the order, then both ran towards the truck.

'Just Bailey!' Daggert said.

Crawford stopped.

'How did you let him get out of the house?' Daggert asked.

'Huh?'

'He must have been in the house, snuck out, and

now he's taken our ride,' Daggert said, shaking his head. 'I don't know who's more incompetent. You, or Bailey.'

'At least neither of us left the key in the car,' he said.

Daggert went to reach for the weapon he'd used on Flo, debating whether to use it on Crawford, but he was distracted by a shout from Bailey.

'There's no key!' she said, holding open the door of the pickup.

Daggert scanned the cottages that dotted the lakeside. 'There must be another car around somewhere. See what you can find,' he told Bailey and Crawford.

Crawford said, 'Even if we get a car, we don't know which way the kid went.'

Daggert again resisted the impulse to shoot him, deciding a phone call he had to make was more pressing. While he was speaking to someone back at The Institute, a rusted old van pulled up alongside him with Bailey behind the wheel.

'Some idiot left the keys in it,' she said through the rolled-down window.

Daggert, phone to ear, raised a finger in the air to silence her.

'I need you to lock in on our car,' Daggert said to someone at the other end. 'No, I do *not* wish to explain why I don't know where it is.'

Crawford opened the side door of the van, waiting for Daggert to finish.

197

'You have it?' he said. 'Fine, now send me the coordinates. And if you breathe a word of this to Madam Director, I shall personally pull your heart out of your chest. Also, there's a possibility we may need backup transportation out of this area if the police get wind of what's been going on. There could be roadblocks. Maybe a chopper or— what? Yes, a boat would work. So long as it's fast.'

Daggert listened for a few more seconds. 'Yes, an hour would be about right. That's good. And have you sent the coordinates? Fine.'

He took the phone away from his ear but did not return it to his jacket. He was waiting for something to show up on his screen, and when it did, he smiled.

'Interesting,' Daggert said, opening the van's passenger door and getting inside. 'The SUV is stopped. The boy hasn't gone far at all.'

He pointed. 'That way,' he told Bailey.

30

When Jeff had left the train station to drop off the garbage at the dump and had got to where the driveway met the main road, he'd made a point of closing the metal and wire gate behind him.

But this time, in the stolen black SUV, he didn't feel he had the time to get out, swing back the gate, drive in, get out again and close the gate behind himself. He had to get off the main road as quickly as possible before Daggert and his pals found a way to come after him. They wouldn't be able to use his aunt's truck, but they struck Jeff as a resourceful bunch who wouldn't be delayed long.

So when he swung the big, lumbering SUV off the road, he drove his foot to the floor and smashed his way through the gate. It made such a huge crashing noise he worried they'd hear it back at the camp. The gate crumpled as it was torn off its hinges, slid across the hood and bounced off the windshield. The glass suffered some cracks, but did not shatter.

Jeff wondered if the glass might be bulletproof.

He barrelled down the narrow, bumpy lane and hit the brakes when the trees opened and the old railroad station came into view. He turned off the engine, snatched the key, jumped out of the SUV and ran for the building, shouting, 'They've found us! We have to get out of here!' as he raced up the stairs.

Chipper whipped his head around and Emily was wide-eyed as Jeff's head appeared behind the banister.

'What's happened?' Emily asked.

'They got Aunt Flo!' he shouted. 'They – they shot her or zapped her or something! I hid in the house! I snuck out the window!'

Chipper got off the beanbag chair and went to him – not so far as to disconnect his collar from Emily's laptop – and nuzzled the side of his leg with his snout in a bid to offer comfort. But Jeff was too panicked to notice.

'Who are you talking about?' Emily asked, now nearly as frightened as Jeff.

'Them!' he said, and pointed to Chipper. 'Whoever's after him!'

Emily's jaw dropped.

'We're not safe here!' Jeff said. 'We have to go!'

'Whoa, whoa, *whoa*!' Emily said. 'What do you mean they shot Flo? Are you kidding me?'

Jeff saw words coming up on the laptop screen, and on the phone in Emily's hand. 'He's saying something,' Jeff said.

Emily looked at her phone and Jeff took a step closer to read the laptop.

I am sorry.

'Sorry?' Emily said.

I made a mistake coming here. I was wrong.

There was a brief pause, and then:

Run.

Emily's eyes met Jeff's. He hadn't known her very long, but he sure had never seen her look that scared.

'Run where?' Emily asked.

Thinking.

'Yeah, well, you better think fast,' she said.

Jeff was feeling so frantic he thought he'd burst out of his skin. They had to do something right now, but he wasn't sure what. At least he had the bad guys' car. He and Emily and Chipper could get in it and take off.

But then what?

Where would they go? What would they do when the car ran out of gas? He didn't know about Emily, but he sure didn't have any money or credit cards. How long would they last?

Not long.

The thing was, they'd last even less time if they stayed here.

Jeff said, 'Emily, they don't know anything about you.'

'What?' she said distractedly. She had gone back to fiddling with her phone and the laptop. She disconnected the cables, including the one that went to Chipper's collar. 'We're wireless,' she said triumphantly. 'What did you say?'

'They know about me, they've figured out somehow I know about Chipper, but they don't know about *you*. You're safe. Take the dog's advice. *Run.*'

'I can't just— I mean, I'm not going to leave you here and—'

'Go,' he said.

She was struggling with a decision, even though she knew it made a lot of sense.

'Give me your phone,' she said suddenly.

'What?'

'Give it to me!'

Jeff handed it over. She connected it to her laptop and began frantically clicking and tapping away.

'I'm setting you up,' she said. 'So you and Chipper can talk. If I leave you with the laptop, they'll be able to trace it to me, and it's too much to carry if you're on the move.'

'Okay,' Jeff said, glancing every few seconds down the stairs.

Tap tap, tap tap tap, tap, click click, tap.

Chipper made an anxious whining noise and was shifting his weight from one side of his body to the other. When The Institute programmed him, they were supposed to make him less susceptible to fear and anxiety.

They didn't do such a good job where he was concerned.

'Okay,' Emily said, disconnecting Jeff's phone from her computer and handing it back to him. 'Now you two can chat.'

Jeff looked at his phone's screen.

I am worried.

'Yeah, you and me both,' he said, looking from the phone's screen to the dog.

Emily was stuffing her laptop into its case. 'I don't care what anyone says, I'm telling my dad. He has to know what's going on. He might be able to help. He's not going to rat anybody out.' Something occurred to her, and she asked for the phone back.

'What?'

'I want to set it up so you guys can talk, but your phone can't be traced. The connection between you two is on, but your phone – as an actual phone – is dead. That should make it harder to find you.'

Jeff wanted Emily to get out of there, but he was going to miss her technical expertise. She handed the phone back to him, slung the computer case over her shoulder, and took a step towards him.

'Be careful,' Emily said. 'When you can, let me know you're okay.'

Jeff nodded. She leaned in and gave him a quick kiss on the cheek.

It was the first time a girl had ever kissed him.

Emily said, 'There's something he wants to tell you.'

Jeff blinked. 'What?'

'I don't know,' she said. 'But it sounds serious. Jeff, he was *looking* for you. From the moment he escaped.'

'That makes no sense.' He looked at Chipper. 'Why is she saying that?' He studied Chipper's face, then looked at his phone.

It can wait. Make Emily go now.

'You better do what he says,' Jeff told her.

Emily scooted down the stairs. Jeff watched from the top as she peered outside first to make sure no one was there, then slipped out the door and was gone.

Jeff looked at Chipper and said, 'I hope you have a plan.'

I do.

'Seriously?'

Chipper nodded.

'Well, out with it then.'

Let them come to us.

31

'Let them come to us?' Jeff said. 'That doesn't sound like much of a plan.'

Chipper circled the beanbag chair, the nails of his paws clicking softly on the wood floor. *If he were a person*, Jeff thought, *this would be pacing and thinking.*

Which was exactly what Chipper was doing. Pacing and thinking.

Let them catch us.

'I'm just a dumb kid,' Jeff said, 'but is your dog brain kicking in a bit too much?'

If a dog could scowl, Chipper scowled. The White Coats had installed more than a few tricks into Chipper, and while he knew they were there, he had never before used them and he didn't know whether they would work. But if they did, he and the boy might have a way out of this.

Or, maybe he should just save the boy. Let the White Coats recapture him. He'd let that happen before he allowed anything bad to happen to Jeff.

You go. I will take care of myself. If they catch me I will be okay.

Jeff swallowed hard. 'That's no plan. I don't want to leave you behind. And anyway, like they say in the movies – don't I know too much?'

I have never seen a movie. But yes, you know too much.

'Then we definitely need a different strategy.'

Chipper's ears stood up. He heard the engine a few seconds before Jeff did. He ran to the small dormer window and looked out. Coming down the rutted road through the trees was a van. Jeff recognised it immediately as Harry Green's car.

Who is it?

'It's okay,' Jeff said, glancing back at Chipper. 'It's a friend of mine. He's parking behind the bad guys' SUV, getting out . . . Oh, no.'

You stole their car?

'Yeah.'

It can be tracked. They can find their cars. They are outfitted with GPS which

'I know what GPS is!' Jeff shouted, slamming the palm of his hand into his forehead. 'I led them right here!' How many times could he be an idiot in one hour? They'd stolen Harry's van and come right after him.

'I'm sorry,' he said to Chipper. 'I'm not really cut out for this.'

He looked out the window again to confirm his fears. But in the time he'd talked with Chipper, the doors of the van had opened, and he couldn't see anyone left inside. Daggert and his helpers, Bailey and Crawford, probably had the railroad station surrounded, getting ready to break in at any moment.

Chipper sniffed the air, confirming to himself that they had visitors. He was picking up three distinct scents. One of them was wearing a flowery perfume.

'We're trapped!' Jeff said. 'There's no way out except to go down the stairs!'

Chipper took a nervous step to the right, a step to the left, then back again. He was worried about whether his plan would work.

We will be okay.

Chipper was not accustomed to giving false hope. He wasn't sure that he had ever been wired to do such a thing, but was that what he was doing now? Was that his canine nature kicking in? Did a dog have the capacity to hope for the best? Were dogs by nature optimistic?

It had been so long since he'd been a simple mutt that he did not know for sure.

And Chipper knew that there was more than one reason he was feeling nervous. It wasn't just the bad people from The Institute closing in on them that was making him anxious. It was the information he had been waiting to share with Jeff.

There are things you should know. Things I have been waiting to tell you.

'Like what?'

Wanted to tell you when we were safe.

'Yeah, well, like my dad used to say, that ship has sailed.'

Chipper glanced about nervously, moved to the top of the stairs so that he could see the entrance.

Years ago, at the beginning of the programme, when they were turning me from an ordinary dog into

Someone was kicking at the door.

what I am now, there were many people involved in the process. White Coats. Some were very mean but some were

The door burst open. Jeff looked down the stairwell and his eyes met Daggert's. Coming in behind him were the other two.

Daggert smiled.

Jeff took one last look at his phone.

nice. More later. Jeff, when I look sleepy, plug your ears. Now put your phone away.

'What?' Jeff said.

Chipper had nothing else to say.

Jeff stuffed the phone into the front pocket of his jeans as Daggert and Co. climbed the stairs. They were careful about it, stepping gingerly on the steps that looked weak.

'Well, look who's here,' Daggert said as he reached the top. He fixed his eyes on Chipper. 'You've had us running all over the place. I'm starting to think maybe terminating you is a mistake. You might be one of our smartest pooches. You've been outsmarting us for some time now.'

His grin grew bigger. 'But not any more.'

His eyes returned to Jeff. 'Thanks for leading us here, kid. Smart move, stealing our car. You might as well have fired off a flare, it was so easy to find you. I'm surprised your legs were long enough to reach the pedals. By the way, I'd like my keys back.'

Jeff dug into his other pocket for them and tossed them at Daggert, who snatched them out of the air as easily as a bat grabbing a bug in mid-flight. The smug look on his face was fuelling the rage Jeff felt growing within him.

And suddenly, Jeff felt himself explode into action, launching himself at the man.

'You killed my aunt!' Jeff shrieked, hammering his fists into Daggert's chest.

The other two grabbed him instantly and hauled him off their boss. Daggert casually brushed off his jacket. Jeff was still carrying some of the dust bunnies from under his aunt's bed.

'Relax, kid,' Daggert said. 'She's not dead. She's out cold, and probably will be for another half an hour or so. We don't kill people unless it's absolutely necessary.' He shook his head in mock sadness. 'Which I believe it will be, in your case. Your aunt won't remember much when she wakes up, and she didn't know that much to begin with. But you, I think, you may know quite a bit.'

Daggert reached into his jacket and took out the device he'd used on Aunt Flo. It had a small dial on the side. He waved it around the room, then focused it on Chipper.

'What I'd really like to do is blow your head off,' he said to the dog. 'Which I've been given the okay to do, if that's what it takes to keep the world from finding out about you. But you've got a lot of valuable equipment in you, and bringing you back intact may just score me some points. So when I zap you with this thing, you'll go to sleep and we'll tie you up tight and get you back to The Institute. But you,' and he turned to look at Jeff, 'are a different matter altogether.' He pointed to the dial on the weapon in his hand. 'When I change the setting on this and shoot you, you'll be dead.'

Jeff said, 'Why was the dog looking for me?'

Chipper shot him a look and wished Jeff was looking at his phone. He would have shouted: SHUT UP.

Daggert blinked. 'What?'

The boy pointed to Chipper. 'He didn't just find me at random. He was *looking* for *me*. Why would he do that?'

Daggert looked genuinely puzzled. 'That's a very good question. Why *would* he be looking for you?' He said to Chipper. 'Maybe, when we get you back, we can hook you up to the computer and ask you a few questions.'

Jeff wasn't going to let on that the phone in his pocket had been set up so he could do just that. But then Daggert looked back at him and said, 'How would you even know the dog was looking for you? Did he *tell* you?'

'Uh . . .'

Daggert took a step closer. 'Did you figure out a way to communicate with this animal?'

Jeff shook his head furiously. 'No! That's crazy! No one can talk to a dog!' He laughed. 'That's the craziest thing I've ever heard.'

Chipper yawned.

'What are you not telling me?' Daggert asked. 'You're holding something back. What's your name?'

'Jeff. I told you.'

'What is your *last* name? Who exactly are you?'

Chipper yawned a second time, and wished he could say to Jeff: *Remember what I said?* He hoped he would remember.

'Conroy,' he said. 'Jeff Conroy.'

'Conroy,' Daggert said. 'Conroy? Did you say *Conroy*?'

Chipper yawned again, even made a small yelping noise as he did it.

The woman said, 'I think we're boring the dog.'

'What?' Daggert said. He looked at Chipper opening his jaw wide for a fourth time.

Jeff looked at Chipper and he *did* remember. He stuck his index fingers into his ears.

Daggert glanced back at him. 'What are you doing? Why are you—'

And then a sound came out of Chipper's mouth that Jeff could not believe. Even with his ears blocked, it was the loudest thing he'd ever heard in his life. A high-pitched squealing noise, like a fire alarm and an air raid siren and a chainsaw all going off at once.

It was so high-pitched that the tiny window he'd peeked out earlier shattered.

Chipper had given Jeff a warning, but Daggert and the other two had none, and before they could even think of covering their ears, their knees went weak and they dropped to the floor.

Daggert let go of the device in his hand as he put his palms over his ears. Once he landed on his knees, he keeled over to one side. So did the other two. They were all screaming, but Chipper was making so much noise it was hard to tell.

Chipper gave Jeff a look, tipped his head towards the stairs, then, like lightning, bolted straight down them.

Jeff was right behind him.

32

'What the heck was that?' Jeff asked Chipper as the two fled from the train station. 'How did you make that sound?'

Chipper didn't want to take the time to explain. He knew that the deafening noise would only put Daggert and his crew out of commission for a few minutes. The priority was to get away.

'Hang on,' Jeff said, running to Harry Green's van to see whether the keys had been left in it. A quick look through the window told him they were not. Daggert wasn't about to make that mistake twice. And with no way to start the SUV, Jeff didn't see that they had much choice but to keep running.

The question was: Head back to the main road, Flo's Cabins, or Shady Acres?

It seemed to him the only option left was to go back to his or Emily's camp and try to get help. They might have been able to give this bunch the slip for now, but they were going to be hard to lose, and for all Jeff knew, they had more people they could bring in to help.

Despite Chipper's warnings, Jeff thought it was finally time to call the police.

'Chipper,' Jeff said, pointing in the general direction of Shady Acres, 'we're going this way. We might be able to get help there.'

That seemed as good an idea as any to Chipper right now.

They ran through the woods, the knee-deep weeds and grasses brushing up against Jeff's jeans and Chipper's furry tummy. The dog had regained much of his strength, bounding almost happily through the foliage, his nose up, taking it all in.

Charging through the woods side by side, Jeff felt an incredible bond with this animal that he had known for only a few hours. Events had somehow brought them together – according to Emily, it was not some random thing – and now the two were shoulder to shoulder, fighting for their lives.

At this moment, there was no one Jeff depended on more than Chipper. His parents were gone, Emily had made a run for it. And even if Aunt Flo was alive, as Daggert suggested, Jeff couldn't count on her for help.

What Jeff did not know was that Chipper felt the same way. He had found the boy, and now he needed the boy's help to stay alive. He was going to do everything he could to make sure the boy stayed safe.

Unless, of course, he became distracted.

They were running together, side by side, when Chipper suddenly veered left. He was like one of those cycles in that old *Tron* movie, making a ninety-degree turn at a hundred miles per hour.

Jeff stopped dead. What had Chipper noticed that he had not? Were the bad guys right in front of them? Were they already at Shady Acres? And if running straight ahead was no longer a safe strategy, why hadn't the dog given him some kind of signal that they had to go a different way?

He didn't have to send him a message on his phone. A simple bark would have done the trick.

Jeff stopped and called out Chipper's name at the same time as he brought out his phone, just in case there *was* a message.

Nothing.

So Jeff started running after him. 'What is it, boy? What's going on?'

He'd lost sight of him. Chipper had dashed off so quickly, the tall grasses had swallowed him up. Where the heck was he?

Jeff heard rustling to his left, then half a second later, darting right past him, inches from his shoe, was a rabbit.

And a millisecond after that, Chipper flew past like a bullet.

'Chipper!' Jeff shouted.

About thirty feet away, the dog's head poked up above the grass, looked back at Jeff.

'What the heck are you doing?'

Words appeared on the screen.

I saw a rabbit.

'Is that rabbit trying to kill us?' Jeff asked, unable to hide his frustration. 'Did he have a gun?'

As Chipper came trotting back, he expressed his regrets.

Sorry. It happens sometimes.

'Sorry? You take off after a bunny and that's all you have to say?'

Do you want to terminate me too?

The words were like a knife to the heart. Jeff dropped to his knees and held out his arms. The dog walked into them and Jeff squeezed his neck. 'I would never, never, ever want to terminate you,' he said.

Good to know.

Still squeezing, Jeff said, 'I think you'd be a great dog without any of your computer stuff. I'd love to hang out here and watch you chase rabbits and squirrels, but right now, we kind of have more important things to deal with.'

That is true. I lost it for a minute.

'Come on.'

They picked up their pace once again, and in five more minutes they were walking – more like sneaking – onto the Shady Acres property. The place was pretty quiet, but Jeff knew there was a chance Daggert and his team might somehow have gotten here before them, once they'd recovered from that sonic boom that came out of the dog's mouth. Emily's dad's truck was over by the house, but Jeff didn't see either of them around.

Jeff had an idea.

'Chipper, instead of trying to steal another car – if we could borrow a boat, get across to the other side of the lake, they'd have no idea where we were. That would buy us some time, give us a chance to figure out what to do next.'

Chipper studied him, then slowly nodded.

That might work.

'Let's head down to the water.'

Jeff made his way across the camp carefully, sneaking around cottages, skulking behind bushes, much like when he was getting out of Aunt Flo's house. He wanted to be out in the open as little as possible.

His back pressed up against a cottage wall, Chipper leaning into his leg, he could see the waterfront, no more than forty feet away. There were three fishing boats tied up to the docks. All aluminium, about four-teen feet long. The outboard motors bolted to the back of them weren't very powerful – no more than ten to fifteen horsepower – and wouldn't get them across the lake in a hurry, but they would have to do. Jeff noticed that Emily's boat was missing.

But then, about a hundred feet offshore, a power-boat appeared. Long and sleek – at least twenty feet, Jeff figured – with a black hull and an oversize outboard motor on the back. Eighty horsepower at least.

There was only one person in the boat, behind the wheel. A man, probably in his thirties or forties. Pretty old, anyway.

Jeff thought if they could flag him down, maybe he'd take them across the lake. They'd be there in minutes.

'Let's go, Chipper,' Jeff said.

Jeff charged out from his hiding spot next to the cabin and ran out to the end of the dock, waving both hands in the air, the way you might try to get a pilot's attention if you were stranded on a desert island.

Chipper ran to catch up to the boy and looked eagerly at the speedboat. Even this far away, he caught the scent of exhaust fumes spewing from the engine. He wagged his tail and let out an encouraging bark.

The boat had been heading straight past, but when the driver saw them he cut the throttle and steered in. As he nosed in to the dock, the motor dropping from a roar to a soft *put-put-put*, the man said, 'Everything okay?'

Jeff had to think of something fast.

'My dad just took off across the lake and forgot his phone!' Jeff said, holding up his own. 'He needs it in case he gets a call from the hospital!'

219

'The hospital?'

'He's a brain surgeon,' Jeff said. 'He's always on call in case someone needs to have their brain fixed.'

Chipper looked up at Jeff as if to say, Seriously? Brain *fixed*? 'Whoa, okay, then you better come aboard,' the man said. 'I can have you over there in a couple of minutes.'

'This is fantastic,' Jeff said, glancing nervously over his shoulder, terrified that Daggert would show up before they could get into the boat.

Jeff reached out to catch the bow so it wouldn't bump the end of the dock and eased the boat around to the side of the dock so he and Chipper could jump in. Jeff got a leg over first, planted it on the sturdy bottom of the speedboat before swinging in leg number two.

Chipper ignored Jeff when he reached out his arms to help him in and leapt through the air into the boat instead.

'This is really, really nice of you,' Jeff said.

'Hey, no problem,' the man said. 'My name's Gordon.'

'Hi, Gordon. I'm Jeff.'

'That's a nice dog you got there. What's his name?'

'Chipper.'

The man said, 'No kidding? That's a nice name for a dog.'

He moved a lever to his side to put the motor in reverse, and slowly backed the boat out into the lake.

Reaching into a small compartment under the dash, he came out with a phone.

'Just got to make a quick call to let someone know I'll be late,' he said.

Chipper and Jeff dropped into a couple of cushy seats just ahead of the motor. 'It's going to be okay now,' Jeff said to his furry friend.

But Chipper wasn't looking at the boy. He had his eyes on the man, and both his ears perked up.

Gordon was speaking into his phone, but with the motor rumbling just behind him, Jeff couldn't make out a word of it.

But Chipper's sense of hearing was right up there with his sense of smell. He listened for several seconds, then turned to Jeff and barked.

'What is it, sport?' Jeff asked.

Chipper barked again and looked at the phone in Jeff's hand. The boy glanced down and saw a new message on the screen.

He just told Daggert 'I got them.'

33

Gordon kept the boat idling about sixty feet offshore.

'You're working for them,' Jeff said to the man.

He turned and smiled. 'Yep. We'll just wait here a few minutes until Daggert arrives.'

They could have jumped out of the boat, but what good would that do? It wasn't as though they could outswim a craft with eighty horsepower strapped to the back of it.

'Please let us go,' Jeff said. 'Please.'

'Sorry, kid. You sit there and don't give me any trouble.'

Chipper and Jeff exchanged glances. Jeff looked like he was losing all hope, but Chipper wasn't ready to give up. Maybe he could try a very simple strategy.

Attack Gordon.

No high-tech gimmicks. No supersonic sounds. He'd just leap at Gordon and bite him. Clamp his jaws on the man's arm and bite down hard, like he did with Simmons. If he could hurt the man, maybe he and Jeff could push him overboard. Chipper was pretty sure Jeff would be able to drive the boat. It wasn't very complicated.

Yes, that's what he'd do. He'd—

Gordon turned the wheel hard, edged the throttle forward, and headed the boat back into shore. Chipper and Jeff turned their heads in unison to see Daggert striding out to the end of the dock. He gave Gordon a beckoning wave. He was still in his fancy suit and his eyes remained hidden behind his pricey sunglasses, but his right pant leg was ripped, and he was limping. Even from out on the water, they could see dark blood stains. Jeff bet that when Daggert was running back down those stairs in the old train station, he went through one of them. He wished the injury gave him reason to be optimistic.

Once the bow was a foot from the dock, Daggert, as delicately as a cat, leaned forward, stepped onto it, and pushed his foot against the dock to propel the boat back out. He stepped over the windshield and planted a foot on one of the two cushioned bucket seats. To Gordon, he said, 'If that dog starts yawning, put your fingers in your ears.'

'Got it,' he said.

Daggert gave Jeff and the dog one of his devilish smiles. 'That was pretty good back there,' he said to Chipper. 'That'll be one of the first things we deactivate when we get a chance. In the meantime, Gordon, you got some tape?'

Gordon reached under the dash and pulled out a roll of duct tape.

Daggert said, 'Wrap up that mutt's snout so he doesn't have a chance to make us go deaf.'

Chipper growled as Gordon pulled off a two-foot length of tape, but when he saw Daggert pointing his weapon at the boy, he allowed Gordon to wrap the tape around his jaws.

Once finished, Gordon asked Daggert, 'Where to?'

'Bailey and Crawford have taken the SUV north to Canfield. We'll follow the lake up that way, then take the dog off your hands.'

'What about the boy?'

Daggert surveyed the landscape. 'We got a whole lake to drown him in.'

'Okay. You're the boss.'

Gordon turned the steering wheel as far as it would go until he had the boat lined up to the north. As he nudged the throttle forward the engine roared into action. The bow began to lift as they accelerated.

'*Jeff!*

The scream came from behind and to Jeff's right. He whirled around and there, about ten feet behind the boat and just off to the side, was Emily in her small aluminium craft. She had it running flat out and was coming up alongside, but as soon as Gordon gave his boat more gas, they'd leave Emily behind.

'*Jump!*' Emily shouted as her tiny boat came up beside them.

Daggert and Gordon glanced back to see what was happening. Daggert shouted to Gordon: 'Go!'

But Jeff had already scooped Chipper into his arms and had one foot on the edge of the boat, ready to leap, when Gordon hit the throttle.

There was no time to think about it.

He jumped. He tumbled hard into the middle of Emily's small boat. He and Chipper hit the bottom with great force, Jeff taking most of the impact on his back. He released Chipper, who leapt over the middle seat to greet Emily. He wanted to give her a big lick, but with his snout taped shut had to settle with nuzzling her with his nose.

'What have they done to you?' she asked, using one hand to pick away the tape while steering the outboard motor with the other. She swung it hard, nearly tossing Jeff back out of the boat again. But it instantly put a lot of distance between them and the speedboat, which was speeding away in the opposite direction.

The speedboat started to turn.

Jeff was thrilled Emily had come out of nowhere to help them, but it was going to be a short-lived rescue. Trying to get away from Daggert and Gordon in her boat would be like a turtle trying to outrun a racehorse.

It wasn't going to happen.

Jeff righted himself and dropped his butt on to the middle seat, facing backwards so he could see Emily and their pursuers.

She had the tape off Chipper and flicked it off her fingers, the wind taking it away.

'Thank you!' Jeff shouted. 'But what now?'

Emily kept a strong grip on the throttle. Her jaw was set tight and her eyes were fixed on something in the distance. Jeff turned to see what she was looking at, but there was nothing but open water. He'd only turned away for a second, but in that time the speedboat had gained on them, big time.

The bow was getting so close that it obscured the view of Daggert and Gordon. It looked to Jeff as though their plan was to run them right over. Maybe Daggert had decided it didn't matter if he got the dog back in one piece. Better to kill them all.

'Emily!' Jeff screamed, pointing.

She didn't look back. She was either really, really fearless, or really, really stupid. Chipper was barking non-stop. Jeff wondered if he'd make that horrible sound again. But would it have any impact over the din of the motors?

The speedboat was only twenty feet behind them.

Chipper had his front paws on Emily's seat to give him a better view of the situation. Jeff took a look at his phone. If Chipper had any great ideas, he was keeping them to himself.

Maybe there was only so much you could expect from a dog. Even a dog like Chipper.

'They're going to hit us!' Jeff shouted.

This time, Emily turned around. But not, as it turned out, to see how close the speedboat was getting to them.

Emily did something that seemed completely, totally, and absolutely insane.

She grabbed hold of the back of the motor with both hands and pulled forward, tipping the motor's propeller, which was spinning at about a million miles per hour, out of the water.

It made a roar so loud it drowned out the speed-boat for a second.

'Emily, what are you do—'

And then Jeff realised. He looked off to the left, and there was the red buoy.

It was the six-foot-tall metal marker that indicated the location of the rock wall just below the surface of the water.

They skimmed right over the submerged wall without touching it. If the motor had been down, there would have been one huge crashing noise and the boat would have come to a jarring halt.

As soon as they'd cleared the underwater fence, Emily dropped the engine back into the water and they kept on going.

Daggert and his friend, however, didn't fare quite so well.

227

The speedboat crossed over the wall at high speed. Chipper and Jeff could barely believe what happened when that eighty-horsepower motor struck the rocks.

The front of the boat kept going. The transom – the back end of the boat – was ripped clean off.

Daggert and the driver pitched over the bow – flying through the air like a couple of massive seagulls – and disappeared into the water. No sooner had they landed in the drink than the front of the boat plowed right over them. The back end exploded. Flames and black smoke shot skyward.

'You did it!' Jeff said to Emily. 'You *did* it!' Jeff was on his feet, arms in the air in victory. Chipper's tail was wagging so vigorously it was making his entire body shake.

Emily steered the boat in a wide arc, heading back in the direction of Shady Acres, while Jeff kept his eyes on the wreckage, waiting to see if one or two heads would bob up above the surface of the water.

They did not.

Chipper barked at Jeff, which he took to mean he had been sent a message. He looked at his phone and saw that Chipper did, in fact, have something to say.

Wow.

34

Jeff wanted to believe they were in the clear, but they still had Bailey and Crawford to worry about.

When Daggert failed to show up in that boat with Chipper and Jeff, his associates would know something had gone wrong. So, even though they were headed back to the relative safety of Shady Acres, it really wasn't that safe at all. The boy and the dog could not stay there long.

As the three of them approached Shady Acres, they saw two men and a woman standing at the end of the dock: Emily's father – John Winslow – and Harry Green, from cabin number eight . . .

And the woman was Aunt Flo!

John grabbed hold of the boat as it reached the dock while Harry secured the front and back lines.

'Aunt Flo!' shouted Jeff, who would have been the first out of the boat if Chipper hadn't leapt out ahead of him.

She had a slightly dazed expression on her face as

she held her arms out to her nephew. As he hugged her, he said, 'I was scared they'd killed you.'

Dozily, she said, 'I'm still not sure what happened. But Mr Green kind of filled me in.'

'I saw the whole thing,' Harry said. 'And I brought John here up to speed, too. Whatever those men wanted, they sure got what was coming to them.' He was looking out across the lake at the still-burning boat.

'What *did* they want?' Emily's father asked.

'Him,' Emily said, pointing to Chipper.

'A dog?' John said.

'You gotta be kidding,' Harry said.

Woozily, Aunt Flo said, 'You know I don't like dogs.'

Together, Jeff and Emily tried to explain what a special dog Chipper was, that he was the product of some secret government research centre. Not surprisingly, the adults were sceptical.

'We can talk to him with our phones!' Emily said. 'I set it all up!'

'Come on, this is crazy,' John said.

Jeff handed John Winslow his phone. 'Ask him something.'

'Ask him what?'

'Anything you want.'

Emily's dad looked dubiously at the screen, then said to Chipper, 'What's three hundred and thirty times four hundred and ninety-one?'

Then, instantly:

162,030.

Emily's dad did a double-take.

Jeff asked, 'Is that right?'

He shrugged. 'I have no idea.'

Emily grinned. 'Trust me, it's right.'

'No, it's a trick,' John said. 'It's the phone answering the question, not the dog. It's an app or something.' He thought a moment. 'I've got a better test.' He handed the phone back to Jeff, then knelt down next to Chipper and whispered something directly into his ear that no one else could hear.

He stood and said to Jeff, 'If he's so smart, he can tell you what I told him.'

Jeff read aloud from his phone, 'Emily means the world to me and I don't want anything to happen to her.'

Emily looked as though she might tear up. She slipped an arm around her father's waist and he drew her tightly to him. The man looked stunned. 'I don't know how this is possible.'

Harry said, 'I think maybe it is, John.'

Jeff held up his phone so the others could see. 'Chipper has more to say.'

They read:

They will be back. With more people.

'What's he mean?' John asked.

'They're going to keep looking for him,' Jeff said. 'And I guess they're going to be looking for me, too.'

'Just give them the dog and tell them you're sorry,' Aunt Flo said. 'Tell them you'll never tell anybody about this!'

Harry put a hand gently on Flo's arm. 'I don't think that's going to satisfy them, Flo. Your nephew's in danger. We have to get him away from here.'

Aunt Flo looked at John. 'Didn't you used to be a police officer? Can't *you* do something about this?'

John looked at her helplessly. 'I've never come up against something like this. But I know some people, I could make some calls and—'

'No,' Jeff said. 'Chipper says these people from The Institute monitor all that kind of stuff. Anyway, I think Harry's right. The part about me – about both of us – being in danger.' He put his hand on Chipper's head. 'But where do we go? How do we get there? I don't know what to do.'

'That's where I come in,' Harry said. 'I'll get you and the dog far enough away that you're safe, and maybe by then we'll have figured out what to do.'

Jeff looked at Chipper. 'How does that sound?'

Okay.

'It's a deal,' Jeff said. 'But how did your van get here? How did *you* get here?'

'I'd seen what they did to your aunt here, and I was hiding behind one of the cabins. One of them – the woman – saw that I'd stupidly left the keys in the van. She took off with it. Luckily, I've got a second set. When they took off up the road, I started to run after them, but I couldn't exactly catch up to a van. A little while later, I heard this crazy, high-pitched noise coming from the woods.'

Jeff pointed to Chipper. 'That was him.'

Harry grinned. 'You got some howl. Anyway, it sounded like it was coming from that old train station.'

'You know about that place?' Emily asked. 'I thought it was my secret.'

Harry grinned again. 'I found it weeks ago when I was taking one of my nature walks. So I headed that way. About the time I got there I saw those three no-goods coming out, one limping pretty bad. Two of them left in the SUV; the one with the limp headed down this way. I went over, got my van back.'

'You're a pretty smart guy," Jeff said admiringly. "You know, I think we should get going.'

'I guess so,' Harry said.

'Can I have five minutes?' Jeff asked. 'Chipper and I have something we have to talk about.'

* * *

Jeff led Chipper off the dock and down the shoreline about twenty yards, where there was a rock about the size of a crushed car. Jeff climbed up on it, sat down, looking out over the water and the dying fire, and patted the stone next to him so Chipper would sit there.

'You had something you wanted to tell me,' Jeff said, phone in hand.

The dog leaned into him, resting his head against Jeff's chest, poking his nose up under his chin.

You remember I said some White Coats were mean and some were nice?

'I remember.'

Your mom and dad were the nicest.

'What?' Jeff put some space between them and looked into the dog's eyes, which Jeff seriously hoped were no longer sending any images back to anybody. 'Are you saying my parents worked for this place, where they turned you into some kind of dog computer?'

Yes. Do you know what your parents did?

'I thought they did research for some drug company.' Jeff felt dizzy, like he could tumble off this rock at any moment. 'Are you sure about this? I mean, you knew their names?'

Edwin and Patsy. They talked about you all the time! You sounded so great. They told me you had a dog and you loved it so much! When your mom and dad were install-ing my equipment they told me about Aunt Flo and how she was the only living rela-tive. I knew if something happened to them you would have to go live with her.

'My parents told you all these things about me?'

They enjoyed talking to me. Not just to see if I could understand language but because they liked me. I could tell they

loved you very much. You had a very nice family.

It was all starting to come together for Jeff. 'So when you escaped, you came looking for me because you knew I'd take care of you. But they must not have told you my aunt hates dogs, that she would never have let me keep you.'

A pause before Chipper said anything.

That was not the only reason why I came looking for you.

'Oh, well, fine – so you *didn't* think I'd be a good one to take care of you.'

I wanted to be sure you were safe. I wanted to tell you what I know.

'So now I know,' Jeff said. 'My parents *lied* to me for years. I thought they were figuring out how to make a new and improved aspirin, but instead they were working for some secret government organisation that turns puppies into – into I don't know what!'

There is more!

'More?' Jeff shook his head. He wasn't sure he could take much more. 'Okay, so what else?'

The other White Coats were worried about your parents. Your mom and dad did not like where the research was headed. They thought the White Coats were going to do very bad things!

'What do you mean?'

They did not tell me. But they made their bosses nervous. Madam Director was afraid of what they might say or do.

'Madam *what?*'

She was afraid your parents would tell the world what The Institute was planning.

'Well, I guess they got lucky when my parents died in that plane accident,' Jeff said. He thought Chipper would have an immediate reply, but nothing came up on the screen. Jeff wondered whether the battery was running low.

But then:

Not an accident!

Jeff felt a chill run the length of his body. 'No, no, no. That was an accident. There were like, dozens of people who got killed. It wasn't just my mom and dad. All kinds of people. Entire *families* got killed when that plane went down.'

So no one would suspect your parents were the target.

'No way. This is crazy! What you're saying . . . what you're saying is . . .'

They killed your mom and dad.

35

The girl in the pink bikini was stretched out on a lounging chair at the end of the dock when she thought she heard some splashing around her. It wasn't that clear, because she had buds tucked into her ears and was listening to music. She had a book on her lap and was working on a tan. If she hadn't had the buds in her ears, she might have heard the explosion further up the lake, and if she had looked up from her book, she might have seen the smoke in the distance.

But the splashing, that she heard.

She closed the book on her finger so as not to lose her place, and looked up.

Coming out of the water was a man in a suit.

Not a rubber wetsuit, like somebody would wear to swim underwater. Not even a swimsuit. It was an actual *suit*. Black jacket and black pants with a big tear in them. White shirt and tie. Even a pair of sunglasses, perched haphazardly on his nose.

The man was, of course, completely drenched as he

emerged from the water. He did not look very happy. He had a gash in his forehead and was bleeding.

The girl took out her earbuds.

'Uh, you okay, mister?'

He eyed her. 'Give me your phone.'

'Huh?'

He pointed to the wires that had been dangling from her ears. 'Are those hooked up to a phone, or not?'

She reached into her lap and brought a phone out from under the book. She handed it to the man. Standing in the water next to the dock, he took it, disconnected the wire and tossed it back to her.

He entered a series of numbers, put the phone to his ear, and turned away from the girl.

'Madam Director,' he said. 'Yes, I'll hold.'

He stood there several seconds, then said, 'It's Daggert.'

'I'm rather in the middle of something,' Madam Director said.

'This is important. It's about the boy.'

'You got him? And the animal?'

'No. And no.'

'That's very disappointing,' said Madam Director.

'The dog was looking for him.'

'Excuse me?'

'The boy. The dog was looking for the boy. The kid's last name is Conroy.'

A pause at the other end of the line. 'Conroy?'

'That's right.'

'The son of Edwin and Patsy?' Madam Director asked.

'I haven't confirmed it, but I think so.'

'That's interesting. That's very interesting. And it's also troubling.'

'It is,' Daggert said.

'You'd better get to the bottom of this, hadn't you, Daggert?' Madam Director said.

'Yes. But I've had a setback. And I have to regroup with my people.'

Madam Director snickered.

'What's so funny?' Daggert asked.

'I am amused,' she said. 'That you should have so much more trouble getting rid of the boy than you did his parents.'

'It'll get done.'

'Oh, I've no doubt of that,' she said. 'If not by you, then by someone more competent.'

'Look, you need to know—'

But Daggert heard a click. Madam Director had ended the call.

* * *

Seated behind her desk, she put down the phone, smiled, and said, 'I must apologise for that interruption. Let's get to know one another. Tell me your names again.'

Two children – a boy and a girl – were sitting side by side on Madam Director's leather couch. Perfectly still, hands folded in their laps. They were no more than seven or eight years old. The boy was dressed in a pair of bright, white running shoes, new blue jeans and a crisp, red, buttoned shirt. His hair was combed neatly to one side. The girl was dressed in similar shoes, pale pink jeans and a white blouse. Her hair was pulled back into a ponytail.

'Let's start with you,' Madam Director said to the girl. 'What's your name?'

'My name is Peggy,' she said quietly.

'That's a pretty name. And how about you, young man? What's your name?'

'My name is Timothy,' he said warily.

'Peggy and Timothy. How nice. What lovely children.' Madam Director smiled. 'I'm so happy to have you here.'

'Can we go home soon?' Timothy asked.

'Why are we here?' Peggy asked.

Madam Director waved her hand, dismissing the questions as unimportant. 'All in good time. But before I answer any of your questions, I have a very, very important one for both of you.'

The children waited expectantly.

Madam Director got out of her chair and came round from behind her desk. She got down on her knees in front of the children so that their eyes were at a level. She took the boy's hand in her left hand, and the girl's in her right and gave each of them a squeeze.

'How would you like it,' she asked, 'if you could be the smartest, most clever, most amazing children in all the world?'

Timothy thought about that and said, 'I guess that would be okay.'

Peggy wiggled her nose around, pondering. Finally, she said, 'It's good to be smart.'

Madam Director said, 'Oh, yes. It's going to be very, very good.'

36

'We should go.'

The voice startled Jeff. He'd been staring at his phone, trying to comprehend what Chipper had told him, struggling to get his head around the significance of those six words.

They killed your mom and dad.

'Hey, pal, we should hit the road.'

He looked up from the phone to see Harry Green standing off to his left.

'We need to get you away from here and come up with a plan,' he said calmly.

'Yeah, right, okay,' Jeff said.

Jeff took another peek at the phone.

The dog leaned in and licked his face.

'How much more is there to tell me?' Jeff asked.

'What?' Harry said.

'Sorry – I was talking to the dog.' He glanced down at the phone.

A lot.

Harry gave Jeff a questioning look. 'Okay. So he does more than solve math problems? He *talks* to you?'

'I can try to explain it on the way,' Jeff said, 'to wherever we're going.'

Harry shrugged. 'You can try, but don't expect me to understand.'

Jeff slid off the big rock and walked back over to where Emily and her father were standing.

'Have to go,' Jeff said.

'I'll probably never even see you again,' Emily said.

Jeff shrugged. 'I don't know. Maybe we—'

Emily hugged him for a good ten seconds, then dropped to her knees to give another hug to Chipper.

He licked her face enthusiastically. Chipper was glad he and the boy were going to stay together, but he was really going to miss Emily. *We might need her again*, the dog thought. *We just might need her again*.

Harry was already by his van, holding the side door open. Chipper and Jeff jumped in and let Harry slide the door shut. They sat side by side in the middle row.

Jeff looked through the window at Emily and sadly waggled his fingers at her. Chipper gave one farewell bark.

Harry opened the driver's door and got settled behind the wheel. He had his own phone out.

'I don't have a fancy GPS system built into the car,' he said without turning around, 'but I got it on my phone. Just going to check the best way to get out of here without going through Canfield. We might get spotted there.'

'Okay, Harry,' Jeff said.

Jeff reached over and patted Chipper softly on the head. 'Whaddya think's going to happen, sport?'

The answer came right away.

I wish I knew.

While Jeff talked to Chipper, Harry looked at his phone.

He was not looking at a map program.

He was sending a text, because even a dog with hearing as good as Chipper's could not tell what someone was saying in a text. It read:

I have them. The boy AND the dog.

Harry put the phone away and said, 'You ready to go?'

'Ready,' Jeff said. 'Thanks so much, Harry. You're the best.'

Chipper chimed in with a thank you bark.

'Hey,' said Harry, 'what are friends for?'

TO BE CONTINUED. . .

ACKNOWLEDGEMENTS

Many thanks to the folks at Orion Children's Books, in particular Lena McCauley and Felicity Johnston, Sarah Heller of the Helen Heller Agency, and at Penguin Random House Canada, Lynne Missen, Kristin Cochrane, Brad Martin and Ashley Dunn.

CAN'T WAIT TO FIND OUT WHAT
HAPPENS TO JEFF AND CHIPPER?

READ AN EXCERPT FROM THE
NEXT BOOK IN THE SERIES,
COMING IN 2018!

They had been on the road for five days.

Harry Green said that was the best way to do things. Keep moving.

'We'll find a different place to stay every night,' he told Jeff and Chipper a couple of hours after they had driven away from Flo's Cabins, the fishing camp on Pickerel Lake where Jeff had been living with his aunt, Florence Beaumont.

They'd had to take off after being tracked down by a team from The Institute. The really scary one was a guy named Daggert. He'd captured Jeff and Chipper and was taking them away in a boat when Jeff's friend, Emily Winslow, saved them. Daggert's boat had blown up, but Jeff hadn't taken much comfort from that. He was quickly learning, from some of the things Chipper had told him, that there would always be another Daggert, even if the original one was out of the picture.

So Harry had volunteered to hide the boy and the dog until they could come up with some sort of plan. Within an hour of being on the road, Harry had taken a screwdriver from the glove compartment, taken the license plates off the van, and swapped them with a car he found parked behind a restaurant.

'There's cameras all over,' he said to Jeff, who was sitting up front in the seat next to him. 'Don't want them spotting our plate. And just to be sure, we stay off the interstates and toll roads. And we won't follow any predictable route. We'll head east one day, south the next, west the next. That way, if someone's trying to track us, if they pick up the scent, they won't say, oh, hey, they're heading that way. We'll be waiting for them. Nope, not gonna happen.'

'What do you think?' Jeff asked Chipper, whose head was between them. The dog had his front paws on the center console, his hind legs on the floor of the back seat. Perched that way, he could see out the front windshield.

A single word came up on Jeff's phone.

Maybe.

Most of the functions on Jeff's phone had been deactivated so that it could not be traced. It could not make calls or connect to the Internet. All it really did now was act as a device to communicate with Chipper, and he could thank Emily for figuring out how to set that up.

'What do you mean?' Jeff said.

We cannot keep doing that forever.

'What's he say?' Harry asked. Jeff told him. 'I'm not saying forever. Just until we figure things out.'

'Why are you doing this?' Jeff asked. 'Why are you helping us?'

Harry glanced over. He looked surprised by the question. 'Are you kidding? Why wouldn't I?'

'You hardly know me,' Jeff said. 'You're just some guy who was renting a cabin from my aunt. You were having a nice summer, going fishing every day. Why put all that aside to help some kid and his dog?'

Harry shrugged. 'Well, first of all, that is not some ordinary dog you got there. Second, I'm retired and don't exactly have any other commitments. And three,' and he looked at Jeff, 'maybe I just cared. I saw a boy in trouble and I didn't see how I could turn my back on him.'

Jeff said, 'I'm sorry.'

'No, don't be sorry.'

'No, I feel bad. You're helping me and I'm not acting very grateful. My mom got mad at me one time, said I didn't appreciate the things other people did for me.'

'I'm sure she wasn't mad at you,' Harry said. 'It's just, sometimes, when you're a kid, you're not aware how much your mom and dad do for you. That's all. I bet, after she got mad, she did something nice for you.

Jeff felt his eyes moisten. 'She took me out for an ice cream,' he said, remembering.

'There, you see.'

Chipper leaned Jeff's way and licked his cheek. Jeff put his arm around the dog's head and gave him a gentle squeeze.

'I think my mom and dad would have liked you,' Jeff told Harry.

'And I bet I would have liked them,' he said. 'You know what I'm gonna have to do? I'm gonna have to get us some cash. We're not going to put a lot of stuff on charge cards, have they figure out where we might be. We're coming up on a little town, oughta be able to get some here.'

Jeff said, 'Where from?'

'A cash machine, where else? There might be a bank, or maybe a convenience store. A lot of them have cash machines.'

That might not be a good idea.

Jeff said cautiously, 'Yeah, but, Harry, I don't know a lot about these things, but if you use a machine, can't they track you just like they would if you used your credit card?'

'Huh?'

'If you use your bank card, and take out money, they'll know. The Institute is probably watching for something like that. And I think a lot of those machines, they have cameras that take pictures of everybody who uses them.'

Harry said, 'Oh, yeah, well, don't worry about that. I got that covered.'

Chipper and Jeff exchanged looks. What was Harry talking about?